Music and Musicians
in Ancient Egypt

Music and Musicians in Ancient Egypt

Lise Manniche

British Museum Press

© 1991 Lise Manniche
Published by British Museum Press
a division of British Museum Publications Ltd
46 Bloomsbury Street, London WC1B 3QQ

British Library Cataloguing in Publication Data
Manniche, Lise
Music and musicians in ancient Egypt
1. Egypt. Music, history
I. Title
780.901

ISBN 0–7141-0949–5

Designed by Andrew Shoolbred
Layout by Charlotte Westbrook Wilson
Typeset in Sabon by Tradespools Ltd., Frome, Somerset
and printed in Great Britain by Biddles Ltd., Guildford and King's Lynn

Contents

Acknowledgements

The present work owes its immediate inspiration to a meeting of the Study Group on Music Archaeology in the International Council for Traditional Music, held in Hanover and Wolfenbüttel in November 1986, to which I had been invited to make a contribution after a decade spent researching other areas of the civilisation of ancient Egypt. I would like to dedicate it to all the participants who with their multiple backgrounds and approaches made the occasion such an eye-opening experience.

I would like to express my appreciation of further detailed discussions on the subject which I had with Professor Ellen Hickmann, Hanover, and Professor Bo Lawergren, New York, though they are by no means responsible for any of the conclusions reached in this book. Last, but not least, I owe a debt of gratitude to Jenny Chattington, my editor at British Museum Press during the early stages, for her interest in the work and for her not inconsiderable contribution towards making it more readable.

Note on musical conventions and terminology

A basic problem in discussing the music of ancient Egypt is the lack of any recognisable theoretical language (see the Introduction for further discussion on this subject). The harmonic theory of Western music, based on the physical laws of harmonics, rests firmly on principles first discovered and propounded by the ancient Greeks. The musical theories of ancient Egypt developed independently; we have little evidence about the absolute pitch of instruments, or whether particular scales were used as melodic frameworks, although we are able to make some assumptions about relative pitch and intervals. For convenience, therefore, modern Western musical terms have been used throughout this book.

Conventional Western music relies on the use of scales, which consist of a given pattern of intervals (the differences of pitch between notes). These intervals are described in terms of tones and semi-tones. Each scale is made up of eight notes (an octave), with a total range of twelve semi-tones. Where intervals are specified in this book they are intended as an approximate guide only, for we can never be certain about the exact tuning of ancient Egyptian musical instruments. The intervals used are as follows, from a given base note:

2nd = 1 tone + 1 semi-tone = augmented 2nd
     − 1 semi-tone = minor 2nd

3rd = 2 tones + 1 semi-tone = augmented 3rd
     − 1 semi-tone = minor 3rd

4th = 2 tones + 1 semi-tone = augmented 4th
     − 1 semi-tone = diminished 4th

5th = 3 tones + 1 semi-tone = augmented 5th
     − 1 semi-tone = diminished 5th

6th = 4 tones + 1 semi-tone = augmented 6th
     − 1 semi-tone = diminished 6th

7th = 5 tones + 1 semi-tone = augmented 7th
     − 1 semi-tone = minor 7th

8th = 6 tones (12 semi-tones: octave)

A scale in which the intervals between the notes are all semi-tones is said to be chromatic.

In Western music the letters A to G are used to designate notes; the interval between each of these notes is a tone, except between B and C, and between E and F, where the interval is a semi-tone in each case. A note whose pitch has been raised (sharpened) by one semi-tone is indicated by the sign #; a note lowered in pitch by one semi-tone (flattened) is shown by the sign *b*. The notes available in classical Western music are therefore:

A, A# (=B*b*), B (=C*b*), C (=B#), C# (=D*b*), D, D# (=E*b*), E (=F*b*), F, F# (=G*b*), G, G# (=A*b*)

1 Harpist. Wall-painting in Theban Tomb no.60 of Antefoker; 12th Dynasty.

Introduction

It appears that long ago [the Egyptians] determined on the rule ... that the youth of a State should practise in their rehearsals postures and tunes that are good. These they prescribed in detail and posted up in the temples, and outside this official list it was, and still is, forbidden to painters and all other producers of postures and representations to introduce any innovation or invention, whether in such productions or in any other branch of music, over and above the traditional forms ... As regards music, it has proved possible for the tunes which possess a natural correctness to be enacted by law and permanently consecrated. (Plato, *Laws*, 656–7)[1]

This quotation from Plato, written in the fourth century BC, brings together the two characters who provide most of the material for this book: the musician and the artist. The ancient Egyptian musician, however, remains a shadowy figure, generally anonymous, and it is only through the artist that we may catch a glimpse of him or her. Without the outline draughtsman, the painter and the sculptor we would know little about the people who played the ancient instruments, many of which have survived. But however much we are thus indebted to the artist, we must nevertheless be aware that he was an interpreter, and that the evidence before our eyes is a secondary source in the study of Egyptian music. The Egyptian artist had one main task: to render his subject in a manner which was to him the correct one. But his aim was not necessarily to produce a naturalistic portrayal in the way that, for example, a modern photographer would. The artist relied on conventions determined at the dawn of history. His concepts had as much to do with empirical knowledge as with a trained eye, and the framework within which he was obliged to work left him little room for improvisation, as Plato noted. Through the millennia new concepts and objects were introduced to the ancient Egyptians, but a considerable period often elapsed before they found their way into the repertoire of the artist.

As music and musicians are our concern, we shall have to question the musical knowledge of the painters and sculptors. Can we learn anything substantial from pictorial representations? Attempts have been made to determine, for example, the musical scales from the distances between the frets in representations of the long-necked lute, likewise intervals from the way a harpist touches the strings of his instrument, or the angle at which a singer holds his arm. Some may feel that musicologists have been too confident in their interpretation of the evidence. On the other hand, we should never underestimate the skills of Egyptian artists, and we are in a position in which we cannot afford but to make the most of the available evidence. While pictorial representations abound and classical authors give an occasional glimpse of musical practices in Egypt, literary sources concerning Egyptian music are in general meagre.

2 A trio playing the lute, harp and lyre, and a dancing-girl, entertaining the tomb owner at his funerary banquet. Relief from the tomb of Ptahmay, Saqqara(?); end of the 18th Dynasty. Egyptian Museum, Cairo.

Most representations of musicians stem from the tombs of private individuals, officials of the king, servants of the gods, workmen and so on. From the 4th Dynasty (*c.* 2600 BC) onwards the Egyptians built or carved tomb chapels over their burial chambers, providing them with extensive wall decoration which would enable the deceased person to survive in the hereafter, when the mummified body had been buried with the proper funerary rites. Egyptian funerary beliefs were complex and multi-stranded, but at every level they were dominated by a common desire to ensure the continuation of the individual's identity after death, and to provide the means of transforming the dead body into a living creature in the hereafter. This is expressed in the decoration of the tombs as well as in the funerary equipment placed in them. So-called scenes of daily life alternate with religious motifs, and although the artistic language changed slowly through the ages, the basic message remained the same throughout the Pharaonic Period. Scenes of agriculture, for example, would come alive through magic, and the farm workers would labour for the tomb owner in perpetuity, supplying his person with material needs. The workshops depicted would manufacture his funerary equipment, as well as tools and objects of daily life. A hunting scene might provide him with game, but it would also in a symbolic fashion keep evil forces at bay. A convivial feast would set the stage for his rebirth, represented by numerous symbols incorporated into the representation. It is in these latter scenes that we find most of the musical ensembles. Temple walls also bear some musical representations, but mainly in connection with public feasts and processions. It is on the monuments of private individuals that we find representations of music as part of the cult of the gods. For example, a singer of the god Amun would set up a commemorative slab portraying himself playing his harp and singing face to face with a deity.

Such representations on public and private monuments are carved or painted with great accuracy and they can tell us a good deal about the instruments and how they developed over time, the techniques used to play them and the types of ensembles that were enjoyed at different periods. Some scholars have even speculated, as we have seen, about what scales Egyptian musicians may have used and the kinds of effects they were aiming to achieve. However, it is the instruments themselves which constitute our true primary source, and they have survived in considerable numbers. Studying the sizes and shapes of these instruments, the materials from which they were made, the arrangements for stringing or the positioning of finger-holes and so on can help to give us an idea of the range of notes and timbres which they were capable of producing. Experiments have been made with replicas of instruments to try to recreate their sounds.

The most important collections of musical instruments are in Cairo, London, Paris, Berlin, Florence, Leiden and New York (see the list of museums on p.137). Most of these objects were acquired during the course of the nineteenth century. They captured the interest of early travellers to Egypt, but although they became treasured items in collections, the circumstances of their discovery were rarely recorded. Most important musical instruments remain unprovenanced unless they were brought to light in more recent times, as for example the splendid lute of Harmosi now in Cairo. Harmosi, whose undecorated tomb was at Thebes, was a singer of the early 18th Dynasty. His lute is of major interest in itself, but its documentary significance is enhanced by the fact that it was found during a properly conducted excavation, next to his mummified body.

The combined evidence of the representations, the ancient instruments themselves and modern versions which still resemble their distant ancestors provides a solid foundation on which to build up a picture of musical activities in Pharaonic times, although some interpretations remain open to discussion. When we come to consider the music itself, however, we are greatly hampered by our lack of information. The paucity of written sources makes it very difficult to judge any theoretical framework. According to Plato (see above), musical theory did exist in ancient Egypt, and was hedged round by a rigid system of laws. Poems and hymns, which are known to have been chanted or performed with some musical accompaniment, may contain clues about musical forms. Patterns of set rhythms or lengths of phrases might be deduced from the words of the text. Repeated lines suggest repeated musical phrases. The wording of a hymn may even suggest antiphonal singing, either by two solo performers, two choirs, or one soloist with choir. Whether the ancient Egyptians practised polyphony in their singing we can no longer deduce, and we can certainly no longer recreate their melodies.

Musical traditions may be passed on directly in an unbroken line from musician to musician, but once the continuity is broken they will be lost to posterity unless they have been written down.[2] The question of whether the Egyptians invented any form of musical notation remains a debatable one. A sophisticated system of writing was in use by the early third millennium BC, and representations of musical activities begin to appear in quantity on the monuments from about 2600 BC. In other ancient cultures with which Egypt is known to have had contacts – in Asia Minor, for example, and Greece and Rome – a kind of musical notation was developed. A cuneiform tablet of the mid-second millennium BC found in Syria contains a hymn which is annotated with interval names and numbers. The Greeks were using the letters of their alphabet for musical purposes by the second century BC, and Greek papyri with such notation have been found in Egypt.

It is difficult to find conclusive evidence from Egypt at such an early date. A more recent source is the liturgy of the Coptic Church. This originated in Egypt, where there was a Christian community from the second century AD. The liturgical language is Coptic, a late form of the ancient Egyptian language. In manuscripts dating from the ninth century and later some musical instructions were noted. Abbreviated words or letters indicate the mode (or scale system) of a hymn, the terminology being borrowed from the Greek. Other geometrical signs written above or between the words have not yet been fully explained: groups of between two and six oblique strokes; groups of between two and five points; and a circumflex. An even earlier series of fragments of parchment manuscripts, dating from the fifth to the seventh centuries AD, appears at first sight to contain a developed kind of musical notation in the form of circles. Some have texts in Coptic and Greek which specifically include musical terminology such as 'tempo' and 'key', so the musical context as such is not in doubt. The words 'beginning' and 'end' are reminiscent of 'da capo' and 'al fine', which, however, have a specific sense in modern Western music. It has been suggested that the rows of circles in twelve different colours correspond to the twelve notes of a modern scale; a more cautious interpretation is that they represent (a) letters, and (b) the planets. Both the Greeks and the Babylonians saw a connection between the planets and musical scales: in Hellenistic philosophy the seven planets were compared with the seven strings of the lyre. The Egypt in which the parchment documents originated was strongly influenced by Hellenistic ideas and philosophy which relate music to the universe. In a hymn dating to the Ptolemaic Period the recipient of cosmic music was Hathor, goddess of music, dance, love and fertility:

> The sky and its stars make music to you.
> The sun and the moon praise you.
> The gods exalt you.
> The goddesses sing to you.[3]

The verse was written on a staircase wall in the temple of the goddess at Dendera; the staircase led to the roof where the image of the deity was carried in procession during festivals.

The concept of cosmic music may, however, have more ancient roots. A representation from the Middle Kingdom (c. 2133–1633 BC) shows a harpist playing a six-stringed harp. The open-air setting is unusual, though not unique. Above his head we see six red disks; there are no inscriptions. A contemporary passage on the wall of another tomb refers to the owner having 'danced like the planets of the sky'. It is just possible that this is rare evidence from the Pharaonic Period of the idea of 'universal harmony' in an astronomical-musical sense, which is expressed more explicitly in later writings. The disks, even if they do not actually represent musical notes, at least suggest musical concepts.

It was in Egypt among the religious sect known as the Gnostics that the 'song of the seven Greek vowels' originated, a mystical chant which was believed to bring the sounds of the seven spheres of the universe into harmony, each letter corresponding to a certain sound. This link between the alphabet and musical notes is a fairly natural one: all letters represent a sound, although some lend themselves to musical sound more easily than others. A writer in the fourth to third century BC, Pseudo-Demetrios of Phaleron, relates that Egyptian priests used vowels in their incantations. The Egyptian language did not record vowel sounds (unlike Greek, which used seven vowel signs), but it did use three weak consonants or semi-vowels: ʿ, 3, w. That the word for 'praise' consisted of these three letters, ʿ3w, may be coincidental.

A scene depicting singers in a Middle Kingdom tomb at Beni Hassan may contain some clues as to which letters might have conveyed musical sounds. Each of two hieroglyphs (í, h) is repeated in a row beside each singer; they have been interpreted as representing the sounds produced by the singers. The row of repeated ʿ signs may either refer to a singing exercise at the end of each phrase, prolonging a particular word (as in Coptic liturgical practice: see chapter 10), or it may signify the length of the entire phrase. The repeated h signs may be comparable to the use of the similarly sounding syllable χε in Byzantine music, which is an auxiliary prolonging a note otherwise sung on a single syllable.

Another scene, in the Theban tomb of Kheruef, dating to the fourteenth century BC, offers further evidence. Over a representation of two pairs of females taking part

3 Clapping ladies at the *sed* jubilee. Relief in the tomb of Kheruef, Thebes; end of the 18th Dynasty.

4 Harpist and chironomist. Relief in the tomb of Werirniptah at Saqqara; 5th Dynasty. British Museum (718).

in a jubilee celebration appear the phrases: 'do with me *hnn*' and 'singing *hnn* repeat [or twice]'. One meaning of the word *hn* is 'rejoice', another is 'halt', and such a phrase could refer, for example, to a rhythmical intermezzo in a chant. However, the letter *n* appears to be written twice, as if to focus attention on a prolonged sound; one phrase even includes the word 'twice' (*sp sn*). The letter *n* is, in fact, ideal for expressing a humming sound, and the hieroglyphs in this scene may be a technical notation of the singers' performance. The hieroglyph for the letter *n* (〰) could even be the precursor of the sign for tremolo which was used in Greek and Latin music, and remains in use even today. It can be no coincidence that in the Middle East the tremolo is executed on the letter *n*.

Recognising that the three letters *hnn* may have been used in a musical sense in ancient Egypt does not bring us any closer to identifying individual notes, but it would seem that they define or describe the quality of certain sounds. Perhaps the most intriguing piece of evidence on the subject of notation is a figurine now kept in the reserves of The Brooklyn Museum in New York (see Plate 1). It represents a seated ithyphallic figure of a man with a harp-playing female perched on the end of his phallus. Other figurines elsewhere depict a similar representation, but it is a matter of considerable interest in this case that the man may have brought the musical score to the performance. A scroll or tablet rests on his lap, the upper surface being inscribed in ink with horizontal lines, partly crossed by short vertical lines. This does not correspond to any system of writing in the ancient world, but it is tempting to see in it some connection with the music performed on the occasion.

Just as Egyptian writing itself is largely pictorial, pictorial representations might themselves contain specific written messages: in other words, the scenes so carefully drawn and sculpted by the Egyptians are to be *read* as much as *contemplated*. This approach has shown successful results in recent years in investigations into the symbolic nature of certain representations, most particularly those concerned with the idea of rebirth. A similar approach led to the most succinct attempt to determine concepts of music as expressed in Egyptian art. It was first proposed by the German musicologist Hans Hickmann (1908–68).

The key to his interpretation lies in a figure who regularly appears in Old Kingdom representations of musical ensembles, the so-called 'chironomist'. Usually a singer, he is shown making specific gestures towards other members of the ensemble (see Plate 2). By comparing these gestures with the positions of the players' hands, Hickmann was able to suggest that the chironomist indicated well-defined intervals to the performer. Whether he acted as a kind of musical director within the ensemble or was a device of the Egyptian artist to represent visually the music being performed remains an open question (see chapter 2).

The following chapters will investigate in detail what the representations and surviving instruments reveal. We shall attempt to focus on the music that could possibly have been played on them, on the occasions on which they were used, and on the persons who were involved in making music, be it for the gods, for kings, for fellow Egyptians, or even, as in the case of the lone herdsman with his flock of goats, for themselves.

1
Music and work

In discussing the role of music two factors of prime importance must be considered: magic and function. Needless to say, a certain element of magic and religion can be detected or surmised in many instances, but the concern of this chapter is music with a specific purpose relating to the daily life and work of the ancient Egyptians.

The performance of music may not be immediately apparent in representations of the type of activity in question, for instruments are not necessarily depicted. Unless the words are actually given, the act of singing may easily elude us, although a person shown with hand to mouth or ear can often be taken to be performing a song or a chant. If we go back to the periods before the emergence of large-scale representations – to the first two dynasties, or even to prehistoric times – the evidence becomes increasingly difficult to interpret; only a small selection of instruments remains to reveal anything of the music of these early people, and we can only speculate about the circumstances in which they were used. Clappers, rattles, jingles and perhaps a flute and an ocarina (a globular flute) may have been used in the cult of a deity, or for a purpose ultimately with a practical aim, like hunting. We can perhaps imagine early man using his voice as well, and not just clapping his hands but slapping other parts of his anatomy to ensure a profitable hunting expedition.

In Pharaonic times we are on slightly firmer ground. A scene from about 1365 BC must have ancient roots: on a relief from a building at el-Amarna a group of women have ventured into woodland to scare birds by beating round and rectangular tambourines. No hunter is in evidence, and the key to the scene's significance may have been carved on an adjoining block. A relief from the Roman Period, now displayed

5 Scaring birds with tambourines. Relief from a building of Akhenaten at el-Amarna. The Brooklyn Museum, New York (60.197.3).

in the Egyptian Museum in Cairo, appears to record a similar event: women beat tambourines to scare birds out of the undergrowth. A boating scene from the Old Kingdom may also show how a musical instrument could be used to flush out water-fowl. A light papyrus boat is being manoeuvred through the marshes by an oarsman and a helmsman, while two men stand up in the boat. A boy holding two decoy birds in one hand blows into a tube. Unfortunately the relief is damaged and the lower end of the instrument is missing, but it has been tentatively interpreted as a trumpet. If so, it would be the earliest example of such an instrument in Egypt, but it may equally well be a megaphone, the trumpet's primitive ancestor, or a reed instrument; it may even be a blowpipe and not a musical instrument at all.

Music was part of the daily life of farm workers, and had a role in the seasonal round of agricultural activities. The Egyptians grew three crops a year, so they had ample opportunity for the displays which traditionally followed the farming calendar. One of the most interesting is the song which was performed when the seed was sown. It is actually about a shepherd: sheep were used to tread the seeds into the soil. If they were used again at the much later stage of threshing, the song would be repeated then. This deceptively simple song has been found above scenes in a number of Old Kingdom tombs, and has been the subject of several learned papers; it has even been argued that it may possess mythological associations.[4] It falls into two parts, in the form of a question and an answer, although it is not clear in which order they will have been performed. In fact, the question of order may not be relevant, for it is more than likely that the song was performed by two groups (or one man and a group, or perhaps two men), each repeating a line for the duration of the song:

Q O West! Where is the shepherd, the shepherd of the West?
A The shepherd is in the water with the fish.
   He speaks with the *phagos*-fish and converses with the *oxyrhynchus*-fish.

The two phrases may originally have been totally unrelated, but may have become joined together because of the common word 'shepherd'. They would possibly have been repeated in an endless cycle – a method of performance well established in other cultures.

During harvest time we find the flautist playing in the fields. A typical example is a relief from the tomb of Kahif at Giza. Unlike his colleagues playing the same instrument at banquets (see chapter 2), he must stand in order to be seen above the vigorous growth of barley. Often one of the farm workers joins in, perhaps placing his sickle under his arm and breaking out into song, one hand to his ear, the other stretched out in one of the gestures made by chironomists in the banquet scenes. Alternatively, he may gather some heads of barley, apparently presenting the bunch to his fellow labourers, or perhaps he is chanting to the barley. It would be interesting to know what he is saying. One clue may be offered by the word 'oxen', which appears in one of the scenes, although this seems to bear no direct relation to the work being carried out. Another scene shows two harvesters going about their business; one says, or sings:

Q Where is the one skilled at his job?

The flautist plays, while the singer with the sheaf replies:

A It is I!

6 Flautists and harvesters. Tomb of Kahif at Giza; 6th Dynasty.

A second adjacent group has a variation:

Q Where is the hard-working man? Come to me!

A It is I. I am dancing.

These examples date back to the Old Kingdom, but evidence from the New Kingdom may be even more enlightening. The decoration in the tomb of Paheri at el-Kâb, which includes agricultural scenes, shows extraordinary similarities with paintings in another tomb that has only recently been published, although it was known to travellers early in the nineteenth century: that of Wensu at Thebes, some sixty miles to the north.[5] Some figures and groups of figures are absolutely identical, as are some of the accompanying texts. What is particularly fascinating, however, is that at Thebes we find the continuation of the speech initiated at el-Kâb. The sheer fact that it was acceptable to give only part of the text suggests that the words do not simply represent ordinary scraps of conversation, however stereotyped, but phrases of a song, or songs, known among farm workers up and down the Nile. The sequence may be reconstructed as follows:

PLOUGHING

Paheri Hurry up with the work, friend,
      and let us finish in good time.

Wensu Now, I shall do more than my work for the nobleman.

Paheri We are hurrying up.
      Fear not for the corn-fields.
      They are very good.

Wensu How excellent is your exclamation, child!
      The day is beautiful.
      free of worries.

HARVESTING

Paheri and Give me a handful!

Wensu   Look, we shall be going home by twilight.

Do not do the tricks of yesterday.
Stop it today!

Later in the sequence of scenes the harvested grain is loaded on to barges, and the texts accompanying the workmen who carry the heavy sacks read:

Paheri and   Must we spend all day
Wensu   carrying barley and white emmer?
              The granaries are full,
              heaps are pouring over the opening.
              The barges are heavily laden,
              the grain is spilling out.
              But one hurries us to go.
              Is our heart of copper?

Apart from words spoken by girls who help collect the ears of grain in the harvesting scene, the utterances can easily be divided into phrases said by two groups of workmen, to be sung alternately as the work progressed.

In Old Kingdom representations groups of men dance while the grain is being taken to the granary. Each beats together one long and one short stick. The significance of this remains somewhat obscure, but it is reminiscent of scenes of the grape harvest which show two men squatting inside a circle, beating together shorter sticks. The circle has posed problems of interpretation, for it does not seem to correspond to any physical location in which the clapping might have taken place, but it may give a clue to the type of performance presented. The Arabic *dâr*, a piece of music with a refrain, literally means 'circle'. If indeed the concept of this musical form does have roots in antiquity, the circle in the grape harvest scenes may be the first graphical representation of it.

7 Beating sticks at the grape harvest. Tomb of Mereruka, Saqqara; 6th Dynasty.

These particular stick-players are not represented after the Old Kingdom, and the next trace of any musical activities connected with the joyful occasion of the grape harvest can be found in the tomb of Petosiris at Tuna el-Gebel in Middle Egypt. Petosiris was a priest during the first years of the Ptolemaic Period: that is to say that as an adolescent he would have experienced the conquest of Egypt by Alexander the Great (332 BC). His tomb chapel has the appearance of a miniature temple, with the scenes on the wall drawing on Old Kingdom tomb decoration, but executed in Greek style, the figures carved in true bas-relief in subtle levels. In a grape harvesting scene we find the following text:

> The gardeners of the vineyard say,
> 'Come our master, see your beds
> and take joy in them.
> The vintners tread the grapes before you.
> Many grapes lie on the ground.
> More juice is in them than last year.
> Drink and get drunk!
> Do not cease to do what you like!
> They have grown for you to please your heart.
>
> Evening arrives,
> dew covers the grapes.
> Let us tread them quickly
> and bring them to the house of our master.
> Everything that is happened through god.
> Our master must drink them happily
> and thank god for them.
> Bring an offering of them to the good spirit of this garden
> so that he may give plenty of wine next year.'

A grape harvest, then, inspired not only a song of its own, or probably a great many which we do not know about, but also, from the movements of the harvesters, a dance. This is demonstrated in the Old Kingdom tomb of Mereruka at Saqqara, where a particular physical exercise is labelled 'pressing the grapes'. It features two girls with outstretched arms, each clasping on either side the arm of another girl who is leaning back off-balance; the entire group appears to be rotating. In the representations the grapes are usually, though not exclusively, harvested by men, but the dance may have as little to do with the real event as the shepherd's song did with sowing. A dance it is, however, for in an adjacent scene is represented the 'mirror dance' performed in honour of the goddess Hathor. There is no indication of music being played in this case, either vocal or instrumental, or of the snapping of fingers or the clapping of hands, but it is hard to imagine a dance without any sort of musical accompaniment.

In the tradition of workmen's songs are also two fragments from the Old Kingdom. One rejoices in the task of carrying the master of the house in his sedan chair:

> Happy are they that bear the chair!
> Better it is for us when full than when it is empty.

The other refers to the fishing net drawn in by the fishermen. While they pull on the ropes and wait for the net to emerge, guessing by its weight and resistance the day's catch, they sing:

It comes and brings us a fine catch!

Noises carry far across water on a quiet day, and it is easy to imagine the sound of the fishermen's song mingling with that of oarsmen in passing ships. In boats with many oars it was essential to keep a steady rhythm, and the easiest way to achieve this was by song. This was so common that it is hardly ever mentioned, except for one famous historical incident. According to Plutarch, on one occasion, when Cleopatra sailed out to impress Mark Antony, the oarsmen had musical accompaniment. But then this was a truly royal occasion: '[the Queen] sailed up the river Cydnus in a barge with gilded poop, its sails spread purple, its rowers urging it on with silver oars to the sound of the double pipe [aulos] blended with [pan]-pipes [syrinx] and lyres [kithara]. She herself reclined beneath a canopy spangled with gold, adorned like Venus in a painting, while boys like Loves in paintings stood on either side and fanned her . . .'.[6]

That a heavy load may be lightened by music is proved in other scenes. In one scene carved on a tomb wall, showing a funeral procession, a group of people drag the coffin to the tomb; to keep them moving at a steady pace and to co-ordinate their movements, an 'instructor' beats two short sticks together in an appropriate rhythm. This may also have accompanied the dancers who, to judge from the decoration on the walls of the tomb chapel, were conventionally present at the funeral.

Another instance also demonstrates the use of rhythm to help in transporting very large and heavy objects. A certain Djehutihotpe from el-Bersha in Middle Egypt had a huge block of calcite ('alabaster') moved from the quarries in the Eastern Desert for a statue of himself. On his tomb wall the block, depicted as a finished statue, is shown being dragged by soldiers. Standing on the knee of the colossus is a man clapping his hands to encourage the soldiers; a companion, who in the picture is almost suspended in mid-air, burns incense to the statue. The shape of the censers is unusual in Egypt, and they are in fact not unlike actual cup-shaped censers used in Egypt some two thousand years later. If they were made of metal they would have made a tinkling sound as puffs of incense were let out.

The daily life of the ancient Egyptians was not all work, but was punctuated by a

8 A queen cutting a trench at a foundation ceremony, with a drum and tambourine being played as accompaniment; 6th-4th century BC. Drawing on papyrus in the Louvre (E 3308).

21

9 Lone flautist under a tree. Relief in Theban Tomb no.69 of Menna; 18th
Dynasty.

10 A fox or a hyena tending his flock; New Kingdom. Drawing on papyrus in the British Museum
(10016).

round of ceremony and popular festivity. Here music also played an important role. At a foundation ceremony on a papyrus scroll of the Late Period (now in the Louvre) a queen wearing the crown of Lower Egypt cuts the first trench for a new building, while a priest recites from a scroll and another pours a libation on the ground. The musical accompaniment consists of a round tambourine, a barrel-shaped drum and hand-clapping, a traditional way of expressing joy and festivity at the beginning or end of a task. In this ritual scene we approach the realm of religious and processional music, which is discussed further in chapters 4 and 5.

The tomb of Wensu at Thebes (see also above) contains a unique scene recording a memorable event in the life of the tomb owner. Usually tomb decoration would depict typical scenes, without specifically recording a particular occurrence. In this instance the ruler, presumably Tuthmosis III, had received a large consignment of goods from the south, some of which he appears to have distributed to the people of Thebes. The items included precious oils and unguents and perishable items such as fruit, vegetables, herbs and fish. The event called for celebration: in the wall-painting a contingent of women has been enrolled to deliver the merchandise; some of the women have brought tambourines, others follow clapping their hands. Wearing scented unguent cones on their heads they run, as the text describes, throughout the streets of Thebes, singing joyfully:

> 'Ointment of sweet moringa oil!
> Unguent of myrrh!'

After the bustle of work or celebration we may catch a glimpse of the lone musician enjoying a moment of leisure with his instrument: a flautist plays in the shade of a tree; another musician blows what is probably a reed pipe. Elsewhere a herdsman whiles away the hours minding his flock of sheep and goats with a pipe cut from a section of rush, probably in the manner of an oboe or a clarinet; it is not possible to tell which, as the mouthpiece is concealed in his mouth. The use of this simple instrument confirms the image of the unsophisticated lifestyle of the shepherd. A satirical papyrus showing animals engaged in human activities depicts a fox or hyena as a shepherd playing a double pipe while watching his flock. If the situation itself is imaginary, the pipe-playing animal with his belongings tied in a scarf on a stick presents a stereotype which the ancient Egyptians would have recognised and with which we may still sympathise today.

2
Popular music in the Old and Middle Kingdoms

Although in this book ancient Egyptian music has been described under such classifi-cations as 'secular', 'sacred' or 'military', and so on, it will soon become clear that these categories overlap. Military trumpets and drums were played during the pro-cessions of the gods; sistra (cult rattles) were shaken by priestesses in religious rituals, but also on occasions associated with funerary rites; and it is largely a ques-tion of interpretation whether the musical ensembles so frequently represented on tomb walls – the main concern of this chapter – should be discussed within a secular or funerary context. Some of these ensembles are specifically labelled 'musicians of the funerary estate', and their function was without much doubt to assist in the transmission of offerings to the deceased tomb owner and his family (see chapter 3).

Although the banquet scenes in which the ensembles are depicted appear to be sec-ular – feasts like those which must have taken place in real life – they represent the 'idea' of a feast rather than any specific event. Right up to the New Kingdom the basic components change little: men and women in their finest outfits; food and drink; music, song and sometimes dance. In the New Kingdom, and in the 18th Dyn-asty in particular, there is a marked change of character in these scenes, which begin to show a wealth of detail with a distinctly erotic significance: lotus flowers, man-drake fruits, wigs, unguent cones, semi-transparent garments, and the gestures of the participants. It is clear that the underlying intention is to create a climate propitious to the rebirth of the tomb owner. Music played a vital part in this process: in the New Kingdom it accompanied songs which expressed the possibility of renewed life

11 Musicians and dancers. Tomb of Niankhkhnum and Khnumhotep at Saqqara; 5th Dynasty.

explicitly; in the Old Kingdom we can trace a similar message in the gestures of dancing girls moving to the music.

In some respects there appears to have been a remarkable degree of continuity in these ensembles over the two-thousand-year period, though there are also obvious differences. Throughout, the harp in its various forms was almost indispensable, and few ensembles were complete without one. Among the wind section we will always find a reed instrument (clarinet or oboe – it is not entirely clear which). In the Old Kingdom the end-blown flute was important, whereas in the New Kingdom the harp was joined by lutes and lyres. For rhythm hand-clapping, a tambourine or, later, a drum could be added. But the voice of the singer, or singers, would be the main attraction. In the absence of any recognisable system of musical notation or documentary evidence, it is only through the study of the surviving instruments and those depicted in tombs while being played that we can gain an idea of what these musical ensembles would have sounded like.

The core of instruments in an Old Kingdom ensemble consisted of harp, an end-blown flute and a simple clarinet (for the two latter instruments, see below). It usually featured one flute and one clarinet only, but it is not uncommon to find more than one harp in a group. One provincial tomb shows seven harps; in another a second flute and clarinet have been added, and in a third we have four flutes, while one scene has no clarinets but two flutes. The recently discovered 5th Dynasty tomb of Niankhkhnum and Khnumhotep at Saqqara near the ancient capital of Memphis has an eleven-man ensemble, consisting of two harpists, two flautists, a man playing an unusually long clarinet, and six chironomists. The ensemble is drawn sitting in a long row, although in reality the arrangement may have been different: the Egyptian artist was not accustomed to rendering perspective, and figures were generally drawn neatly side by side. A wooden model of an ensemble dating from the Middle Kingdom has a harpist sitting on either side of the tomb owner and his wife, while three girls sit facing one another at his feet clapping and singing.

Ancient Egyptian harps can be divided into two groups: arched and angular. The angular harp was probably a later import and only became common during the New

Kingdom, but the arched harp seems to have been a native instrument, known from as early as the 4th Dynasty (*c.* 2613–2492 BC). There were various forms of arched harp, but the type used during the Old Kingdom is generally referred to in the literature as a 'shovel-shaped' harp, which aptly describes the appearance of its wooden body. The Egyptian name, *bnt*, was also used for other types of harp. The 'shovel' was covered with a membrane to provide an enclosed shallow space. The inside surface of the shovel, concealed from view, sometimes had painted decoration. A wooden suspension rod passed across the membrane from the lower end of the neck and served as a means of attaching the strings. At the upper end of the instrument the strings were wound around the neck; immovable pegs ensured that they did not slide downwards when the instrument was in use. An overall tautening of the strings could be effected by moving the suspension rod downwards, but the final tuning of the individual strings must have been done by twisting the knot around the neck. The number of strings generally varied between five and seven, but some harps had eight, nine, ten or even twelve. The instrument came in various sizes, but was always played with the base resting on the ground, the player kneeling or squatting behind it. Harps of this type continued to exist well into the New Kingdom (two such instruments are in the British Museum), but they disappear from the representations with the end of the Middle Kingdom.

In the ensemble from the tomb of Niankhkhnum and Khnumhotep (mentioned above) the two harpists play shovel-shaped instruments. The right-hand harpist is depicted entirely in profile, but an attempt has been made to show the sound-box of the other harp from above; unfortunately the draughtsman did not complete the design to show the second 'wing' to the right of the suspension rod (this way of drawing a harp is more evident in other contemporary representations). Both of the instruments here would have had nine or ten strings: it is often difficult to count the number of strings, especially when, as was usual in the Old Kingdom, the scene is carved in relief – do we count the incised lines or the spaces in between? The normal technique of playing this harp would be to pluck the strings between thumb and index finger using a pinching action. The harpist on the right pinches a string in this way with his left hand, while his right hand is placed below, with the fingers spread out. As his right hand is touching a different group of strings we must assume that he is playing another note with it, although he is not using the pinching technique in this case. Experiments with replicas of ancient harps have revealed that the strings were placed so close together that only the slightest touch would produce a clear note with no interference from the neighbouring strings. Hence the pinching technique would seem to have been the most practical if a clear note was the goal. However, can we be sure that this was the case? Here, sadly, we are hampered by our ignorance. The clarinet, as we shall see, produced two notes so close together as to be almost one, and it may be that the harpist would have striven for a similar effect. In any case, from the present evidence there is no way of telling whether the two notes played by our harpist would have sounded simultaneously or one after another.

Part of the relief has been damaged, and the left hand of the second harpist is missing, but his right hand appears to touch a string, though it is impossible to tell which of his fingers he is using. However, he is not shown pinching the string, and though we cannot be more precise the two harpists are obviously using different techniques. They are both touching the same string on their respective instruments, although this does not necessarily mean that they are playing in unison. It is apparently no simple matter to arrive at an exact tuning of this type of harp, and one is once again left with the feeling that unison and perfect pitch were by no means the object.

Other representations can give us further clues on the technique of playing the harp. For example, in the tomb of Idu at Giza five harpists perform with a flautist, a singer and a chironomist. The positions of two of the harpists' hands are particularly interesting and unusual (second and third players from the left): while the right hand plucks, the other presses against the same strings lower down, towards the sound-

12 (*above left*) Harpists. Detail from the relief in the tomb of Niankhkhnum and Khnumhotep at Saqqara; 5th Dynasty. See Fig.11.

13 (*left*) Harpists. Tomb of Idu at Giza; 6th Dynasty.

box, so low in fact as to press them against either the suspension rod or the covering membrane, thus effectively shortening the string by perhaps a few centimetres. There can be little doubt that this was a means of providing an additional range of notes. The strings of an Old Kingdom shovel-shaped harp varied little in length, so the scale available on open strings must have been roughly chromatic, but by using the technique demonstrated by the musicians in the tomb of Idu a wider range of notes would have become possible. It is not certain that this technique was in general practice; it may have been a last resort of the musician whose instrument had not achieved the proper initial tuning.

The second component of the standard Old Kingdom ensemble was the end-blown flute (*m3t*); it changed little in appearance during the course of Egyptian history and a similar instrument, known as the *nây*, is one of the most popular instruments in Egypt and North Africa today (see chapter 10 and Plate 2). Flutes found in Middle Kingdom burials are just under 1m long, with a diameter of 1.8cm or so. This seems to correspond to the overall dimensions of flutes depicted on Old Kingdom monuments. The sound was produced by blowing across the upper edge of the instrument, which was held in an oblique position. Unlike its modern counterpart, the ancient flute had few finger-holes, usually just three or four positioned at the lower end of the instrument. By overblowing a fair range of notes could be obtained, although we do not know if these possibilities were fully exploited by the ancient musician. Like the shovel-shaped harp, the *m3t* vanished from the banquet ensembles at the end of the Middle Kingdom, but it reappeared in ritual music and it undoubtedly continued in popular use.

The reed instrument in these ensembles (*mmt*) has generally been identified as a single-reed type, that is to say a clarinet, although it is by no means clear from the representations or from surviving examples what kind of mouthpiece would have been used. The instrument is virtually identical in appearance to the instrument used in modern Egyptian folk music in that it consists of two parallel tubes of equal length tied together, the knots secured with resin. Each tube has a separate mouthpiece consisting of a thin tube, closed at the upper end; into this a tongue is cut and vibrates in the player's mouth. Unfortunately, no ancient mouthpieces have survived, and when the instrument is shown in use the evidence is concealed in the player's mouth. It is peculiar that when depicted as a hieroglyph, and thus not being played, the instrument has no mouthpiece at all. The clarinet had four to six holes along the front of each tube. It was usually played in a horizontal position, or slanting slightly upwards, the fingers of each hand simultaneously covering opposing holes. This would have produced a double note, often with a slight variation of pitch, but with a loud, rich tone.

However, the automatic identification of the instrument depicted as a clarinet should perhaps be treated with some caution. In theory it could have been played with a double reed, in which case we would be talking of an oboe rather than a clarinet; the distinction between the two types of mouthpiece would not have been very obvious in a small hieroglyphic representation and reeds separated from the rest of the instrument would have had little chance of being noticed by the early archaeologists. Only very few oboe reeds have survived, and these are no earlier than the New Kingdom. Musicologists use the internal diameter of the tube to arrive at a theoretical distinction between clarinets and oboes: an instrument with an internal

14 Clarinettist and chironomist. Tomb of Nenkheftka at Saqqara; 5th Dynasty. Egyptian Museum, Cairo (CG 1533).

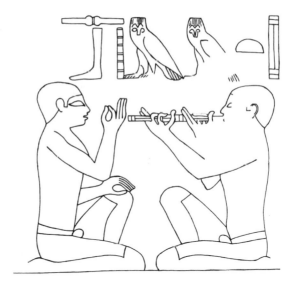

diameter of less than 1cm is taken to be an oboe; a wider bore will suggest a clarinet (or even a flute, if the tube is incomplete). Clarinets, judging from the representations, were shorter than oboes, although there are exceptions. Surviving tubes of clarinets are between 25.1cm and 31cm long without their mouthpieces, and they have a bore of between 1.1cm and 1.4cm, but tubes found out of context and often in a fragmentary state are not always easy to classify, and they are almost impossible to date. The best way of identifying an instrument as a clarinet must be to detect traces of the string and resin with which the tubes were tied together.

In the ensemble from the tomb of Niankhkhnum and Khnumhotep, besides the two flutes, there is a third instrument which presents a few puzzles. Although it is labelled *mmt*, it is unusually long for a clarinet. It is possible that the sculptor made a mistake in depicting this instrument and such an error could have been rectified later by a covering of plaster. However, the downward slope of the instrument suggests that this length was intended: the musician would have had difficulty in holding such a large instrument in the conventional horizontal position for long. However, comparison with a modern instrument may offer a solution to this conundrum. The Egyptian clarinet today exists in two versions: the *zummâra*, which has its vibrating reed cut from the lower end of the mouthpiece, and the *mashûra*, with the reed cut from the upper end. The *zummâra* articulates most readily the high notes, obtained by overblowing, and the best result is achieved with the instrument held in a horizontal position. Lower notes are more easily produced with a *mashûra*, which is held at a downwards-sloping angle, as in our scene. The length of the instrument here suggests that low notes are being played, although it is puzzling that the finger-holes are positioned on the upper half: if no further holes were provided (the wall is damaged where the second hand would have been positioned, so it is impossible to be certain), the intervals that could have been obtained would have been reduced.

The study of representations in the tombs can complement that of surviving examples and tell us much about the capabilities of these ancient instruments, but most importantly they offer clues about how they were played, and even about the kinds

29

15 Clarinettist. Detail from the relief in the tomb of Niankhkhnum and Khnumhotep at Saqqara; 5th Dynasty. See Fig.11.

of effect aimed at. Old Kingdom scenes in particular present a wealth of evidence on musical practices. The key is a figure who features regularly in ensembles of the Old Kingdom: the chironomist, literally 'one who makes signs using the hands' (see Plate 2). It was Hans Hickmann who first presented an interpretation of the part this individual played in the representations.

The chironomist presided over the group and, by a range of gestures, appears to have determined the pitch and intervals on which the musicians based their performance. In some cases the chironomist seems to be singing, but in this respect he may differ little from a modern conductor miming the notes and willing the orchestra to produce a particular quality of sound. The short texts written above the ensemble refer to the action of the players: 'striking the harp', 'blowing the pipe', and so on. The chironomist is said to be 'singing' to the harp, flute or clarinet. The word for 'singing' is qualified by a hieroglyph in the form of a human arm, not, as we would perhaps expect, with an ear or pair of lips. But to a deaf person today a gesture would immediately suggest a substitute for sound, and as far as ancient music is concerned we must indeed use our eyes rather than our ears.

A group of musicians would often be served by more than one chironomist: apparently they might have one, two or, in an extreme case, three each. This rather confuses the neat explanation of the chironomist as a kind of music director. Would more than one chironomist actually have been present at a musical performance? Perhaps this was the draughtsman's way of conveying to us, the spectators, what we cannot hear: a method of demonstrating visually the range of notes struck, not necessarily simultaneously but during the course of the performance. This may then be the earliest attempt at musical notation. Another factor may lend weight to this suggestion: the chironomist appears regularly in Old Kingdom ensembles, rarely in those of the Middle Kingdom, and disappears entirely in the New Kingdom. If his role within the ensemble was as essential in real life as the Old Kingdom scenes suggest, we may wonder how the musicians of the later periods could have managed without him. If on the other hand the gestures of the chironomist made no sense to the musicians after the Old Kingdom, the artist may have left him out when depicting a motif so obviously inspired by the musical performances of his own time.

Hickmann analysed the chironomists' gestures, and compared them with the positions of the musicians' hands, especially those of the harpists. The basis for his calculations was the fact that a string of any given weight and tension will vibrate at double the frequency of another exactly similar string twice its length; the shorter string will produce the same note an octave higher. Stopping a string halfway along its length by a finger will create the same result, as the vibrating length of the string is halved. Other intervals are created by reducing the vibrating length of the string to different proportions. Thus the positions of the musicians' hands enable us to make some calculations about the intervals, based on a study of the vibrating lengths of various stringed instruments depicted in the representations. This entire scheme presupposes absolute faith in the accuracy of the ancient draughtsman, but there is in fact some consistency in the depictions, and a relation can be presumed between particular chironomic gestures and the fingerings shown.

The tomb of Niankhkhnum and Khnumhotep was discovered after Hickmann's death, and it is interesting to apply his method of interpretation to the musical scenes depicted in it. The five musicians are accompanied by six chironomists. Three of them sit facing the harpists. All have one hand placed on their knee, which must indicate the beating of a rhythm or measure, but the position of the other hand differs in each case. The man in the centre holds his hand to his ear, a gesture much used by Oriental singers, enabling them to alter the sound of their voice inside their head, and thus to adjust it to create the desired effect. According to Hickmann, the gestures of the two other chironomists – one with outstretched palm and the other holding his hand with the thumb and index finger together – may represent two points in a musical scale, the steps in between possibly being indicated by the inclination of the arm. A standing figure at the extreme right encouraging the ensemble to get on with the singing of 'the one about the two divine brothers' is an unusual addition. He holds the thumb and index finger of one hand together, and this third chironomic sign may also be directed towards the harpists. Correspondingly, three notes appear to be played on the harps. The right-hand harpist plucks the second longest string with his left hand and touches three of the shorter strings with his right. The second harpist also appears to be playing on the second longest string with his right hand. It would thus seem that the sign of index finger and thumb held together (given twice) signifies the lower of two notes in an interval, for in two instances it is the long strings which are struck. Unfortunately, as the left hand of the second harpist is missing, the evidence here is inconclusive.

From the evidence of such representations Hickmann supported that it might be possible to recognise the interval depicted as a fifth, the outstretched palm representing the upper note, the gesture of thumb and index finger held together indicating the lower. The same signs can be recognised in the tomb of Ptahhotep at Saqqara, where a chironomist gives two signs to a harpist, one showing the outstretched palm, the other holding thumb and index finger together. The harpist plays two different notes: his right (lower) hand pinches one of the shorter strings, while the other, placed above, apparently plucks one of the longer strings.

Scenes such as this one also provide tantalisingly incomplete evidence on whether the ancient Egyptians practised polyphony: is is clear that two notes are being indicated and played, but we cannot tell whether they are being struck simultaneously or

16 Harpist and chironomist. Tomb of Ptahhotep at Saqqara; end of the 5th Dynasty.

one after another. The details of this little picture are of crucial importance, but we need corroborative evidence for a full interpretation and this is not yet forthcoming.

The scene in Niankhknum and Khumhotep's tomb allows us to compare the chironomic gestures given to the harpists with those directed towards the two flautists. Two chironomists perform signs with their right hands which seem to correspond to the first two steps in the flute's scale: the right-hand flautist appears to cover all the finger-holes, whereas the left-hand one leaves the bottom hole open. The chironomists' gestures are similar to those described above, although the angles of the arms differ, so the interval played by the two flutes must correspond to that between the second(?) and sixth(?) strings of the harp. This implies that the intervals between individual strings on the harp must have been fairly small: four strings seem roughly to equal one finger-hole on the flute. It is perfectly possible to reproduce an ancient flute and work out the distances as represented by the draughtsman, but this experiment, interesting though it would be, could furnish no definite proof about the actual scale used by the ancient musicians. We must think in approximate terms only, and any more precise statement should be considered with caution. The Egyptians themselves may have worked within a very flexible framework. The research of Diodorus revealed the existence only of a high, a low and a medium tone in Egyptian music (see below).

According to Hickmann, a relief from the tomb of Werirniptah at Saqqara may offer some rare evidence about rhythm: it shows a harpist and a flautist, each with a singer/chironomist. Although the angle of their arms differs, each chironomist performs a similar gesture with the right hand: the hand is held up, the palm towards the musician; the third and little fingers are bent over, covered by the thumb; the middle and index fingers form a 'V'. The flautist's chironomist beats his knee with the fist of his left hand, while his colleague's other hand is not in evidence at all. The chirono-mists' gestures are reminiscent of a technique of counting much used in Asian and Middle Eastern societies. In traditional Indian dance music it is specifically used to count the beats. If this is what the chironomists are doing here – counting a rhythm, rather than indicating the line of a melody – it may offer further clues about musical form. As mentioned in the introduction, we have no direct evidence that the ancient Egyptians used specific musical forms, although we may infer that they did from hymns and songs which have survived. However, this enigmatic scene strongly sug-gests that their music did have regular countable beats, and hence a specific musical form which could be analysed and categorised. Unfortunately though, the interpre-tation of this gesture must remain conjectural, as it is very rarely represented.

The musical ensembles depicted in Old Kingdom tombs are frequently shown in proximity to dance scenes, but it is not clear whether the instrumental music is actu-ally accompanying the dancing. Different registers may suggest a different environ-ment or a different occasion, or they may be the artist's way of arranging a greater number of participants at a specific event. There are instances where, for example, two harpists perform directly in front of a group of dancers, or where a mixed ensemble, including two female harpists, play in a similar situation. In the latter case the musicians are without their singers or chironomists. These troupes of dancers are generally all female, and they are invariably accompanied by persons clapping their hands in a rhythmic or melodic fashion. The dance was usually the one called the *ibȝ*, of which two typical steps are depicted: one shows the dancers with one foot lifted slightly above the ground and both arms above their heads (though sometimes just one arm is lifted); in the other, reminiscent of the modern can-can, the girls lift one leg right up while their arms are stretched out in front of them. In one tomb it is indi-cated that song, dance and hand-clapping are part of the same performance: immedi-ately above the dancers a row of hieroglyphs records fragments of the words sung in

17 Flautists. Detail from the relief in the tomb of Niankhkhnum and Khnumhotep at Saqqara; 5th Dynasty. See Fig.11.

honour of Hathor (see chapter 4). The raised arms may originally have symbolised the horns of the goddess. It is worth mentioning that the same gesture occurs in African fertility dances, and we may have here the first precursors of festive scenes which become so significant in later periods (see below).

The dance was performed to delight the tomb owner's *ka*, his personality or spiritual force, one of the elements which continued to exist in the afterlife, but only if proper nourishment were forthcoming and, it would seem, relief from boredom through entertainment. With his habitual economy, the sculptor reveals little about the setting, although one artist in the provincial cemetery of Deir el-Gebrawi in Middle Egypt wanted to show that a garden was the proper place, where dancers would perform to the sound of a harp. The participants in all these activities are mostly anonymous, but from time to time the tomb owner's children or grandchildren are given a part to play. If the owner were a member of the royal family the dancers are said to come from the 'harim'. Elsewhere they seem to have some connection with the embalming house, and they must thus have been professional funerary dancers.

The Old Kingdom began to decline towards the end of the 6th Dynasty around 2181 BC. In the period of disorganisation that followed there is little visual evidence for music, although it must still have been played. By 2133 BC the 11th Dynasty was inaugurated at Thebes, and during the course of the Middle Kingdom (11th-12th Dynasties) our sources in art and literature begin to find a voice again. In the decoration of provincial tombs of this time music has a far less prominent position, though this may not necessarily reflect a decline in the art in the capital, where the evidence is more scarce. The 'banquet music' of the Middle Kingdom appears to be an extension of that of the Old Kingdom, some scenes evidently deliberately archaising and harking back to representations of some five hundred years before. Again, we are left at the mercy of the draughtsmen, who were perhaps following ancient models rather than the fresh evidence of contemporary music.

It is in the provincial cemetery of Meir in Middle Egypt that we find the closest parallel to an Old Kingdom ensemble, where a male harpist, flautist and singer/chironomist perform together. In another tomb at the same site a female ensemble includes a flautist, a harpist, a woman clapping her hands and one possibly singing. Apart from the unusual sight of a female flautist, the harp in this scene is a novelty: instead of the conventional Old Kingdom shovel-shaped harp, this one has a strongly curved neck, as well as a deeper sound-box, and it seems to have some decoration at the tip of the neck. This is a rare, early glimpse of the 'ladle-shaped' harp which became common in the New Kingdom. It is regrettable that no actual ladle-shaped harp has survived complete; all that remain are one or two decorative heads which may have come from the necks of harps of this type. It would indeed have been interesting to be able to study the construction of the bowl-shaped sound-box and the characteristic 'curl' at the lower end of the suspension rod.

The new harp, with its strongly curved neck and deeper sound-box, would have required a different technique for playing and it would have produced a new quality of sound. The strings are now set at a much wider angle to the suspension rod; they may be almost perpendicular. The musician was no longer able to shorten a string by pressing it against the membrane. The difference in the lengths of the open strings was not necessarily more marked, for the curve of the neck was counterbalanced by the attachment of the strings at the sound-box at a more or less even level. The ratio between the longest and shortest string in two harps represented at Beni Hassan is approximately 3:4, giving a theoretical range of half an octave. Shared between seven strings, this interval would divide into a scale that would probably have been roughly chromatic. In order to produce substantially different notes, if this were indeed desired, the musician would have had to shorten a string by pinching it firmly with one hand, while at the same time avoiding interfering with neighbouring strings. We have no way of knowing to what extent the musician adjusted the final tuning through the tension of the individual strings.

Even in the tombs at Beni Hassan in Middle Egypt, which boast the most extensive programme of decoration of that period, scenes of instrumental music are sparse, being restricted to a female duo of harpist and singer, and a quartet consisting of a female and a male harpist and two singers or chironomists. The harps depicted here are all different: perhaps the artist was struggling to represent new forms of the instrument from life, rather than blindly copying the models of his predecessors. It is interesting to note that one of the harps is decorated at the tip of its neck by a human head, a custom which was just beginning at this date.

At Thebes only one tomb of the Middle Kingdom has survived with any substantial wall decoration, even though the city was gaining prominence as a religious centre at this time. In the tomb of the vizier Antefoker are four excellent representations of harps in two separate scenes. In both a man and a woman are shown playing side by side. In one case their harps are identical in size and appearance, differing only in the details of their decoration. In the second scene the woman's instrument is

18 Harpists. Tomb of Amenemhet, Beni Hassan; 12th Dynasty. British Library (Hay MSS 29813,20).

about three-quarter size only. The harps are of the Old Kingdom shovel-shaped type with five strings each, but the necks of the instruments anticipate the curve of later variants. The same couple play at the banquet in both pictures, and are identified as the singer Didumin and the songstress Khuwyt, called in to entertain the vizier in perpetuity with their songs about Hathor, the golden goddess, and about the vizier himself, wishing him life and health.

With these Theban harps the ratio of the shortest string to the longest one is approximately 2:3, indicating an interval of an augmented fifth. As this interval is divided between five strings, the scale is no longer roughly chromatic, but would have had larger steps, including some full tones, though the exact subdivision must remain conjectural. It may be an interesting exercise to work out the ratios of the individual strings, but such calculations would be misleading, as unknown factors such as the thickness and tension of the strings of individual instruments would considerably affect the tuning of the instruments and hence the scale or scales in use. In the few instances where fragments of strings remain on surviving instruments, information about their thickness is rarely available. The three strings on a lute in the Cairo Museum have a diameter which 'varied around one millimetre'. Since the tuning is essentially dependent on the tension of the strings, any calculation based on the length of strings has practical value only where one string is concerned. The degree of accuracy by the draughtsman would also have to be taken into consideration. However, we can say that a basic system of tuning must have been in operation, for three of the harps have a large number of pegs – nine (or eight, if we count the spaces between the lines) – compared to the five strings of the earlier types.

The four representations of musicians in the tomb at Thebes show identical methods of playing the harp: the strings are plucked with both hands, and none is shortened to alter the pitch. But the technique has changed since the Old Kingdom: now the players use thumb, index finger and middle finger, while the remaining two fingers are bent towards the palm of the hand, out of sight. In each case two strings are touched by each hand, either simultaneously or one after the other. Thus for each harp a total of four notes are sounded, leaving just one string unaccounted for: in one scene it is the middle string of both harps, in the other scene it is the shortest string of one harp and the longest of the other, the three-quarter sized harp.

Antefoker's tomb contains other representations of music and dance, and the festivities commemorated include dancing to the accompaniment of hand-clapping and the sound of one-handed clappers. Two of the performers could almost have been taken from a banquet ensemble: a female flautist and a songstress or chironomist with a scrap of a song written between them: 'Come, Sobk [a crocodile god], to Antefoker, that you may do as he fancies'. The songstress holds one hand to the ear like her male colleagues of the Old Kingdom, while the other is directed towards the flautist with fingers outstretched. The flautist, covering all the finger-holes, plays the lowest note available on her instrument. These scenes were painted for the vizier's delight in perpetuity, but Antefoker's expectations were dashed, for his wife took over the tomb and the vizier himself was buried at the other end of the country.

Although music had a less prominent place in Middle Kingdom tomb decoration than ever before or after, the Egyptians of this period appear to have appreciated it as much as ever. It is a sign of the musician's prominent position that single harpists are depicted on commemorative stelae set up by private individuals (see chapters 4 and

19 Flautist and chironomist. Theban Tomb no.60 of Antefoker; 12th Dynasty.

9), and occasionally the harpist is part of a small ensemble. One stela shows a male harpist and three hand-clapping ladies, all of whom are mentioned by name; and on another we see a lady 'singing to the harp' which she is playing, three females 'singing with the arm' (i.e., while clapping?), and a scantily dressed girl jumping in the air with a branch in her hand, an exercise described as *ksks*. This little scene is of great interest, not only because of its inscriptions, but also because two different techniques for clapping the hands are shown: with flat palms and with rounded palms. As a quick experiment will easily reveal, the quality of sound is quite different.

In the latter part of the Middle Kingdom there is evidence that influences from abroad were making themselves felt in the musical life of Egypt. Certain new types of instruments which became common in the representations of the New Kingdom are first seen during this period – for example, a portable boat-shaped harp and an early representation of a lyre, also found in one of the Beni Hassan tombs, although no actual example survives from this date: a painted scene shows a group of foreigners arriving in Egypt with their womenfolk and donkeys. They have the appearance of bedouin from Asia: the women wear patterned garments in vivid colours which contrast strongly with the customary white dresses of the Egyptians. A bearded man has brought a treasured possession from the country he has left – his lyre. This instrument is identical to lyres shown in representations from the lands on the northeastern frontier of Egypt. The Egyptian artist at Beni Hassan has studied his subject well, and the very accurate drawing even includes the arrangement of a group of strings running at an angle to the strings being played. This must be an early example of 'sympathetic strings' known from more recent stringed instruments. In Egypt the lyre was to become very popular; it was played particularly by women and it remained in use until the end of Pharaonic times. The draughtsman from Beni Hassan was a pioneer; only one other artist appears to have captured this novel subject at such an early date, in a clay model of a lyre-playing woman. But like the bedouin from Beni Hassan, she also appears to be a visitor from foreign parts.

Other intriguing evidence that foreigners may have introduced new instruments during the late Middle Kingdom has been discovered in the ruins of a palace in the city of Avaris in the Delta.[7] During the course of the 13th Dynasty merchants and artisans from the areas of Phoenicia and Canaan arriving in Egypt had settled there, and early migrants built their dwellings in the ruins of an old palace. One of these

20 The 'Beni Hassan' lyre-player; 12th Dynasty. British Library (Hay MSS 29853,272).

was found on excavation to contain a set of three hand drums. They are of a type known in modern Egypt as *darabukka*, a clay pot open at the lower end, with a membrane glued or laced to the upper rim. This drum is scarcely represented in ancient Egypt. One wall-painting shows a cup-shaped drum which appears to be of this type, and two clay pots with membranes have been recorded, but these are not open at the bottom end. The three drums from Avaris are all vase-shaped in the sense that they are roughly hemispherical with a narrow projecting lower end. Their fragmentary state prevents complete measurements, but the upper diameter of the first is 14.2cm, and that of the second 16.2cm; the second drum has a lower diameter of 5.8cm, and the third 4.3cm. The second drum is 11cm high. The drums are thus quite small and can easily be carried in one hand. The upper edges are perforated with holes; a crescent-shaped slit in the second drum may have served as a sound-hole.

A search through material from contemporary settlements elsewhere in Lower Egypt by the excavator, Manfried Bietak, brought to light other items of pottery which may now be classified as drums. A copy of the largest of the Avaris drums was fashioned by a local potter. According to Bietak, a membrane with medium tension produces good results, especially when using the technique of beating the edge of the instrument. The modern *darabukka*-player excels in alternating such high-pitched notes with deeper ones obtained by hitting the centre of the membrane. With the drums at Avaris was found a scraper made of bone. In its fragmentary state it is 16.7cm long, and has parallel incisions across one side. The sound would have been produced by scraping across the ridges with a stick. It is difficult to explain the purpose of the instruments found at Avaris; Bietak suggests a cultic or ritual function. Information from the homeland of the settlers is equally sparse.

When the administration of Egypt disintegrated towards the end of the Middle Kingdom the foreign settlers assumed control, first of the north-eastern Delta, then of the entire country. During the Second Intermediate Period, Avaris became the capital of the so-called 'Hyksos' kings, but when they were driven out by native rulers life seems to have continued much as before in Egypt. Although some of the foreigners' introductions were undoubtedly retained – the horse and chariot were the most important – it is not certain whether the Hyksos were responsible for the appearance of new musical instruments, and the origin of the innovative types which became characteristic of the New Kingdom remains an intriguing but unsolved problem.

3
Tradition and innovation in New Kingdom and Late Period music

Representations of music-making in the Middle Kingdom had been relatively sparse and uninformative, but the New Kingdom marks a complete contrast, both in the quantity of available evidence and in its scope. The majority of the surviving tombs of the period are at Thebes, and the musical scenes on their walls are rich and varied. Throughout the whole of the New Kingdom (except for the brief interlude at Amarna; see chapter 6), Thebes was the centre for religious affairs, while government was administered from Memphis in the north. It is only during the past decade or so that some of the contemporary tombs of officials at Memphis have come to light. (One scene discovered earlier is reproduced in Fig. 2). Many remain to be cleared, and there is a long way to go to redress the balance of information from the two sites.

In the 18th Dynasty 'banquet' scenes are an essential part of tomb decoration, and few tombs lack a picture of the tomb owner and his wife seated at a well-stocked offering table; rows of men and women take part in the festivities, dressed in their finest clothes and adorned with unguent cones, necklaces and lotus flowers. The participants are rarely shown eating anything, but wine and beer are passed around, and it is a matter of course that for a perfect party entertainment is provided in the form of music and, sometimes, dance. The core of the ensemble generally consists of harp, lute and double oboe, occasionally with additional instruments such as lyre, tambourine and different kinds of harp. The single wind instrument would have provided a powerful melodic element against the background of stringed accompaniment. The instrumentalists could be joined by people singing and clapping their hands.

We have already seen how during the course of the Middle Kingdom the harp underwent some changes. By the New Kingdom quite specific forms of the instrument were in use. The harp found in virtually all ensembles is the so-called 'boat-shaped' harp. It stood almost as tall as the player, though slightly smaller versions also existed. The instrument had a gently curving outline and a U-shaped hollow sound-box covered with a membrane, which had spotted painted decoration, imitating the skin of an animal. The sound-box was cut flat at the lower end, but tapered gradually towards the neck; the decoration of a lotus flower concealed the joint between the neck and the body of the instrument. There were usually nine to twelve strings, secured between pegs at the neck. This type of harp had no other adornment in the form of heads of kings or deities; in fact, it seems to have had no religious connotations at all. Considering its obvious popularity, it is curious that not one example, or even part of one, has survived.

This harp differed in many respects from earlier instruments. It was much larger and produced lower notes. It usually had more strings, and thus a greater range of available notes; and the curve of the neck meant a more marked difference in the lengths of the strings, so that the instrument's span may have been in the region of two octaves. It is easy to imagine how the wealth of notes which suddenly became available must have enriched the music of the time.

The boat-shaped harp appears to have developed on Egyptian soil, probably from the shovel-shaped harp. Its earliest trace is a wall-painting from a tomb decorated in the early part of the reign of Tuthmosis III (c. 1480 BC), but the actual date of the painting may be even earlier, as the tomb owner, Ineni, was an official under the two previous kings too. The harp shown in Ineni's tomb is a small version. Although it has six pegs, only four strings are in evidence. It is played resting on the ground in an upright position, with the musician standing behind. The membrane has the natural coloured markings characteristic of this type of harp. An instrument discovered in a Middle Kingdom burial at Beni Hassan (now in Liverpool) may be a forerunner of the boat-shaped harp. Although it is just 87cm long, it had the flat end of the large instruments and the hull-shaped body. The surviving suspension rod carries notch marks for five strings.

The full-sized boat-shaped harp, being such a large instrument, must have been heavy and clumsy to transport, but a smaller variety was available which was light enough to be carried on the musician's shoulder. This is known as the portable boat-shaped harp or shoulder harp. Several instruments of varying sizes survive in museum collections and we are able to examine in detail their construction. One example in the British Museum is in exceptionally good condition, for most of its membrane survives. Two groups of four sound-holes are pierced alongside the lower end, with two more near the neck. Another harp in the same collection has lost its membrane, but this enables us to examine the inside. Neck and body are made of one piece of wood, the lower half being hollowed out to provide a cavity. In contrast to those of its larger relatives, the instrument's sound-box is rounded at its lower end, not flat. A small knob projects into the sound-box to fasten the suspension rod, which was attached at its lower end by a piece of string through a hole in the membrane. The rod was thus brought into close contact with the membrane, which had the effect of amplifying the sound of the strings. Experiments on a modern replica show that the loudest sound is obtained when the rod is in close contact with the skin, but not too close to the knob. On the harp in the British Museum the reconstruction of the strings and rod has not been entirely successful, since the suspension rod no longer touches the membrane, but it is evident how the arrangement should have been.

The maker of another instrument of the type, now in Cairo, was exceptionally fortunate in having at his disposal a piece of sycamore wood which provided body and neck as well as pegs in one piece. The resulting instrument, 50 cm long, is a work of great beauty, for the carver has exploited the nature of his raw material to the utmost. The oval sound-box was covered with a membrane nailed in position, and the neck of the instrument was carved in the shape of a ram's head. The entire instrument was painted white.

The portable harp usually had four strings, fastened to pegs at the upper end as before. The modest curve of its neck means that the technique of playing could, in theory, have been the same as for the harps of the Old Kingdom, which had a rather similar outline and small intervals between the notes obtainable on the open strings. A study of one of the representations shows that the ratio between the shortest and

the longest of the four strings was 5:6. Such a small difference suggests notes close together. A particular feature of these harps is the slightly waisted shape of their bodies. This may have been an unintentional result of the tension of the membrane, for the walls of the sound-box had no supporting devices to prevent warping. On the other hand, the waisting may have had a purpose: these instruments are, after all, distant ancestors of the violin and guitar, and the question becomes even more relevant in relation to lutes (see below).

In the representations the portable harp is shown held in a rather insecure position while being played, and it must have been no simple matter to keep the instrument balanced. Sometimes the lower end of its neck rests in the hollow between the player's neck and shoulder. It seems as if the player plucked two strings in identical fashion, but in one instance the player's fingers are intricately linked with the strings. The musician holds her instrument horizontally, perfectly balanced, and there can be no doubt that the artist has captured a master harpist at work.

Although the portable harp was used on secular occasions, it did not inhibit the musician from chanting a verse to a god while playing it. Indeed, most of the songs performed at banquets were dedicated to a deity, usually Amun, in whose honour the greatest annual feast in the Theban necropolis was celebrated. The performer could even be a 'singer of Amun'. One such was Amenmose, son of Bakt, who owned a splendid instrument, now in the Louvre. It carries an inscription which includes a line of a poem to Amun: 'Sweet is the air you give, Amun, O sweet of air'.

The portable harp, popular with men as well as with women, did not remain in favour for as long as we should perhaps have expected for such a useful little

21 (*left*) Musicians. Theban Tomb no.38 of Zeserkaresonb. From left to right: large boat-shaped harp; lute; dancing girl; double oboe; lyre; clapping ladies. 18th Dynasty. British Library (Hay MSS 29851,257–60).

22 (*below*) Early examples of a ladle-shaped and a boat-shaped harp. Theban Tomb no.81 of Ineni, now largely destroyed; 18th Dynasty. British Library (Hay MSS 29822,87).

instrument, of which so many examples have survived. It appeared in the representations in the reign of Tuthmosis III and vanished less than a hundred years later. Perhaps its limited register of notes was found too restricting, although this was remedied in one isolated case: one instrument, now in New York, has no fewer than sixteen strings, but the idea seems never to have caught on.

The ladle-shaped harp, sporadically seen in the Middle Kingdom, became a well-defined form which eventually appears to have developed into several varieties, changing shape all the time. It is this harp, in all its forms, which became the instrument of the solo harpist (see chapter 7), but for a long time it was part of the banquet ensemble, played mostly by men, though also occasionally by women. No actual instrument has survived, and this hampers our investigation. The most distinguishing feature of this harp is its deep sound-box. The Egyptian artist represented its shape as approximating a semi-circle, but as he did not attempt to work with perspective we are left with only an educated guess as to what he meant in this particular case. The decoration always emphasises the rounded part of the sound-box with a semi-circular floral ornament, and this is the only clue we have to suggest a hemispherical shape. In theory, the sound-box as represented could equally have been oval, wedge-shaped or as 'boat-shaped' as any of the other harps. A similar problem occurs when discussing the giant lyre of the Amarna Period (see chapter 6).

23 (*above left*) Girl playing a portable boat-shaped harp. Theban Tomb no.17 of Nebamun; 18th Dynasty.

24 (*above right*) Girl playing the ladle-shaped harp. Theban Tomb no.100 of Rekhmire; 18th Dynasty.

The neck of the ladle-shaped harp rises in a steep arch to a position almost at a right angle to the plane of the sound-box, which the strings meet at a wider angle than in any of the harps described above. The tip of the neck is more often than not decorated with the head of a falcon, a goddess or a king. The instrument is usually shown on a stand, which appears to be attached to the sound-box with a curled piece of wood, the lower end resting on a leg shaped like the hieroglyph representing an 'Isis knot'. The sound-box itself was thus not in direct contact with the ground. When not in use, the harp tilted forward to rest on a level part of the stand. The harpist is shown squatting or kneeling behind the instrument.

The ladle-shaped harp had between seven and eleven strings, most frequently nine. In a painting in the Theban tomb of Rekhmire the strings can easily be measured and the ratio between the shortest and the longest is about 2:3 (an augmented fifth). Divided among some ten strings, this would in theory give an average interval of less than a semi-tone. Another harp, in the tomb of Nakht, suggests even closer intervals (ratio=5:6). By far the most common way of playing this type of harp was by pinching two notes separately, the player grasping a longer and a shorter string with each hand. Again, there is no way of telling whether or not the two notes would have sounded together polyphonically.

The earliest true ladle-shaped harp is shown in two wall-paintings in the tomb of Ineni. In one it is played by a harpist accompanied by three women clapping their hands; this version has six strings and nine pegs. On the opposite wall the same musician performs on an instrument with seven strings and as many pegs; alongside a man plays the earliest known boat-shaped harp (see above). In pitch the ladle-shaped harp fell between the boat-shaped harp and its portable version. Since harps of precisely this size came to be used to accompany songs, the pitch must have been particularly suitable for the purpose. Although we cannot know how the harp sounded with the voice, we may be able to piece together some evidence by analogy with other instruments: the deliberately uneven tuning of the two tubes of the clarinet, for example, and the close intervals of the stringed instruments. Perhaps this was the very effect which the musician aimed for and the public liked to hear. The popularity of the ladle-shaped harp and its successors may be due to the fact that it complemented the sound of the human voice in a way that the Egyptians found pleasing.

The harp, as we have seen, had a long history on Egyptian soil, but other instruments were more recent introductions. The lute, for example, had been known to the Babylonians some thousand years before it appeared in Egypt around the turn of the 18th Dynasty. Its Egyptian name is not established beyond doubt, although there are two possible candidates. The word *gngnti* is suggested by its similarity with the name of a modern African instrument, but it appears only at a late date in Egyptian history. The word *ntḥ* might also be considered; it occurs in a New Kingdom text describing frivolous music-making, a context in which the lute would fit perfectly. The determinative used with the word ($\sim$) clearly indicates that the instrument is made of wood – the harp sometimes includes a similar sign in its spelling.

The lute that the Egyptians adopted was the long-necked type. The sound-box came in different forms, but in the 18th Dynasty it was most commonly either made of a natural tortoiseshell or carved from wood in an elongated oval shape (see Plate 5). The sound-box was covered with a membrane, occasionally provided with holes. The entire instrument might be red, or the wooden part might be whitewashed. The

25 Two types of lute in one scene. Wall-painting from Theban Tomb of Nebamun; 18th Dynasty. British Museum (37981).

straight neck passed between the membrane and the sound-box and, piercing the membrane at intervals, it continued to the opposite end of the sound-box. The upper end of the neck was sometimes decorated with the head of a goose or duck, a falcon, the head of a goddess or that of a king. There were two or occasionally three strings, each tied around the upper end of the neck with a separate piece of cord, the ends of which fell in tassels. At the other end they were attached to a small wooden device which could be moved to tauten the strings and tune them all at once. They were lifted from the body of the instrument by means of a bridge, which in the representations shows up as a white triangle. The lute was played with a plectrum, though for special effects this could be discarded and the fingers used instead. In a wall-painting in the British Museum, the plectrum hangs from the body of the lute while the lute-nist's thumb has just struck the strings.

In contrast to those of the harp, the resounding strings of the lute were all the same length. On a magnificent instrument, now in Cairo, the three strings are of equal weight, which suggests that they would have been tuned approximately in unison. To produce notes of different pitch the player would have shortened the vibrating lengths of the strings by pressing them against the neck. The ancient Egyptian lute-nist was an accomplished musician, able to produce a great many notes. The evidence for this comes in the form of frets, transverse marks on a few representations of lutes. It is difficult to be precise about the intervals which these frets may indicate, but it seems certain that they were close together. A lute depicted in the Theban tomb of Nakht has been carefully examined by Hans Hickmann, who concluded that the six frets (plus one hidden behind the musician's hand) produced the following intervals: 134C, 114C, 341C, 202C, 264C, 207C (100C=1 semitone). On other lutes, as for example those represented in a fragment of wall decoration from Thebes now in the British Museum, the frets are much closer together. In one case eight frets are visible, and these begin halfway down the neck; in another some seventeen frets can be made out, again suggesting very close intervals. Experiments on a replica of the Cairo lute suggest that the musician may have found it difficult to cover all three strings with one finger when shifting from one note to another. The intention may, therefore, have been to cover one or two of them only and to leave the remaining string (or strings) as a drone.

Towards the end of the 18th Dynasty some lutes begin to show a slight waist. This is particularly evident in one of the reliefs from el-Amarna, an interesting early example of waisting on a stringed instrument. Lutes were played by men and women. They usually appear in ensembles with other instruments, although occasionally they are shown played by a solo performer.

Another foreign import, the lyre (*knnr*), undoubtedly came to Egypt from Asia, like many portable objects probably first brought by bedouin tribesmen and other travellers. During the course of the New Kingdom we meet variant forms of the lyre first seen being carried by a bearded man in the tomb at Beni Hassan. The instrument basically consisted of a sound-box from which project two arms, joined at the top by a yoke. The representations show between four and nine strings, though some surviving instruments have provision for as many as thirteen. The strings were attached at the upper end to the yoke. Strips of cloth or papyrus, or sometimes wooden pegs, were inserted into the knots to facilitate the tuning and to ensure that the strings remained in tune while the lyre was being played. At the lower end they were fastened to a metal hook or inserted into holes along the upper edge of a wooden box which was in turn fixed to the sound-box.

The quality of the sound was influenced by the sound-box, which was basically square or trapezoid in outline. The internal arrangement of the sound-box varied. Several extant instruments demonstrate this. In some only the lower part of the sound-box is hollow, and it is open at the lower end. Other lyres have a board at the bottom, which is pierced with sound holes, though in some cases the board is nearly solid. The thinner the walls of the sound-box, the more freely they vibrate and the better the sound becomes.

The arms of the lyre might be straight, shaped like papyrus columns, or they might curve strongly, sometimes even resembling the figures 5 and 7. They might also have the decoration of a goose's or horse's head. In Egypt both symmetrical and asymmetrical lyres were known, although only the asymmetrical form was in use as early as the 18th Dynasty. Several asymmetrical lyres have survived. They range in height between 26.5 and 73cm. One bears an inscription to Amenophis I (1546–1526 BC); if this instrument were to date from his reign it would be the earliest surviving lyre, but unfortunately we cannot be certain of this, as Amenophis was deified towards the end of the 18th Dynasty and many votive objects were subsequently dedicated to him. This particular example measures 54cm in height and 32cm in width.

26 Harpist and girl with Bes-tattoos holding a lyre. Theban Tomb no.341 of Nakhtamun; 19th Dynasty.

As its name suggests, on an asymmetrical lyre one arm curves more strongly than the other, but this does not automatically mean a greater variety in the lengths of the strings. Sometimes the yoke is attached parallel to the sound-box and string-holder, and the difference would therefore have been minimal. The curved arms were not merely a decorative element, but must have offered this form of lyre a further advantage: ease of playing. By extending one arm of the instrument to make the yoke wider than the sound-box, the latter could have been kept fairly lightweight. While in use these instruments were held with the strings in an almost horizontal position. The player brushed most, if not all, of the strings at once with a plectrum, while deadening some of the other strings from behind with the spare hand. The pressure of the fingers may have also stretched the strings and thus altered the pitch: this technique, used in modern African folk music, can be clearly recognised in the ancient pictures, though as far as the tuning is concerned we are left in the dark. In some asymmetrical instruments the yoke is no longer parallel to the sound-box, and this would allow for a greater difference in the lengths of the strings, resulting in a larger range of notes.

The oboe (*wdny*) seems to have been known in the Sumerian city state of Ur in Mesopotamia around 2000 BC. When, by the beginning of the New Kingdom, it was introduced into Egypt it took the place of the clarinet in banquet ensembles, and was invariably played by women. The instrument consisted of a pair of tubes made from natural reed, with a mouthpiece of two pieces of rush inserted into the upper end of each tube. There were finger-holes at the front and sometimes thumb-holes as well. The oboe differed from the clarinet in that its two tubes were not tied together, although some musicians held them in an almost parallel position when playing. Others preferred to hold them at an angle, which facilitated overblowing. Surviving instruments vary in length from 20 to 59cm, and similar variations in size can be seen in representations during the course of the New Kingdom. The bore is usually 6–7mm, the walls being as thin as 0.5mm; surviving reeds are from 5 to 8cm long. The professional oboe player would keep a selection of tubes of slightly different lengths in a box, along with rushes for making reeds and a lump of resinous paste for tuning. A variation of only a fraction of a millimetre in the size of a finger-hole on a wind instrument can affect the pitch, but it is possible to compensate for small inaccuracies by adjusting the air pressure when blowing: a musician becomes accustomed to the weaknesses of his instrument. For this reason it is not possible to measure distances between finger-holes on surviving wind instruments and expect to find the exact scales used by their owners, and in any case thousands of years of desiccation will have altered the pitch. But it is of course possible to obtain an approximate idea of the intervals and available notes. The number of holes along the front of the tubes ranges from three to seven, though a few have eleven. Some have as many as three holes on the back, though not all of these were necessarily meant to be left exposed. An awkward thumb-hole would probably have been blocked to correct the tuning or to cover an error in the manufacture. In contrast to modern wind instruments in the Western tradition, the finger-holes on any given tube were identical in size, which suggests that the basic concept for a subdivision of the scale was mathematical. Unfinished instruments reveal that the finger-holes were marked before the upper end of the tube was pierced through and a mouthpiece fitted. The initial division must thus have been carried out visually. The end result was, again, a roughly chromatic scale.

The two tubes of an instrument might vary in length, either marginally (two matching tubes in the Louvre are 53 and 53.5cm long) or substantially. One tube might have fewer holes than the other, in which case it would undoubtedly have served as a drone; one hand was placed considerably lower than the other on the second tube, and in one representation the musician clearly exposes two finger-holes with her right hand. But the musicians might also use more intricate fingering techniques, as for example in a wall-painting from the Theban tomb of Nebamun, now in the British Museum. The higher notes are played with the right hand on the left tube, the lower with the left hand on the right tube. The double reed is remarkably clear in this painting, freshly cut and placed on the lips of the musician. In fact, the reed would actually have been concealed in her mouth while she played.

Hand-clapping and other rhythmical effects sometimes accompanied the music in the ensembles. A rectangular tambourine came into use at about the same time as the portable boat-shaped harp. An impressive specimen was discovered at Thebes in the burial of the mother of Senmut, Queen Hatshepsut's famous architect. The instrument measures 74 x 39.9 x 6cm. It was covered on both sides with a membrane, a fact not immediately obvious from the representations. The edges of the tambourine are slightly concave. In fact, the tambourine found its greatest popularity in street music (see chapter 9), and is only depicted in ensembles half a dozen times over some eighty years. It was always played by women, held fairly high and resting in the hollow of the left elbow.

The ensemble is sometimes joined by a young girl who performs dance steps,

27 Oboist and dancers. Tomb of Nebamun; 18th Dynasty. British Museum (37948).

waves one-handed clappers, or holds her hands to her breast as if concealing a small object in her palm – a jingle perhaps (see Fig.29). We should mention that some of the instrumentalists (although never the players of the large harps) are also shown moving their feet. The lutenist is particularly mobile, and may even twist her body to face in the opposite direction.

No banquet music was complete without the human voice. By the New Kingdom the chironomists shown in Old Kingdom scenes have vanished, but the singers remain; they were probably the *raison d'être* of the ensemble in the first place. The spirit of the music they played is suggested by the songs which the ancient artist has rendered in hieroglyphs among the figures. We see stray verses of favourite songs, as for example:

> Come, O north wind. I saw you when I was in the tower.

> Can it be [the goddess] Maat
> in whose face there is a desire for getting drunk?

> Unguent on the locks of Maat, for health and life are with her.[8]

> The beauty of your face shines, you appear, you come in peace.
> One gets drunk by looking at you,
> You who are as beautiful as gold, O Hathor.
> May I be given a fresh mouth with the water you have provided.[9]

> Ptah has planted this with his two hands to please his heart.
> The pools are full of water, the new land is flooded with love of him.[10]

A serious note is struck in other songs, but the intention is obviously to entertain the tomb owner in the Hereafter:

> Very prosperous may they be,
> the years which the god has decreed that you shall spend.

May you spend them endowed with favour, in health and joy . . .
in your mansion wedded to eternity and linked with endless time.[8]

The Amarna period, those few years when Amenophis IV, later known as King Akhenaten (1367–1350 BC), moved his capital to his new city of el-Amarna on the east bank of the Nile, marked something of a break with the traditions of the past. The music of this fascinating period will be discussed separately in chapter 6. When court and officials returned to Thebes and Memphis, they put the religious and artistic revolution of Akhenaten behind them, but in some respects it was not easy to pick up the threads. By far the greater part of our information about the 18th Dynasty stems from a tradition of tomb decoration which included, even glorified, secular music by virtue of its part in funerary beliefs. With the advent of the Ramesside kings at the beginning of the 19th Dynasty this came to an end, though it does not necessarily follow that musical activities ceased or altered a great deal. Now scenes depicting ensembles are few and far between, although the representation of solo harpists reaches a peak. Because of this change in subject matter the tradition of secular music after the Middle Kingdom has barely been carried forward to posterity, for we are left with at most half a dozen scenes which can be said to have a bearing on the kind of music which is the subject of this chapter. Just two scenes of 'banquet ensembles' have as yet been recovered from the Memphite area in the tombs of the late 18th Dynasty and Ramesside Period. One of these, a fragment of a relief found reused in a neighbouring monastery and now in the Cairo Museum, indicates that music was still thought to be a suitable topic for tomb decoration after the Amarna Period: one man plays a harp, another a lute which may be the pear-shaped instrument known from the Late Period (see p.54).

At Thebes the tomb of Paraemheb, possibly of the early 19th Dynasty, contains a banquet scene with harp, lute and lyre, but the tomb is unpublished and at present inaccessible. The tomb of Bekenamun shows a modest scene of a girl playing a lute adorned with a duck's head, accompanied by a dancing girl with single-handed clappers; a third scene in the tomb of Nakhtamun has a harpist and a lyre-playing girl (see Fig.26).

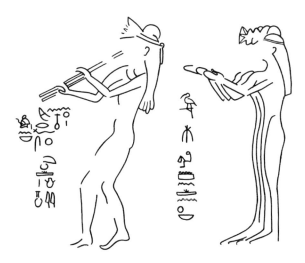

28 Oboist and clappers.
Theban Tomb no.342 of
Dhutmosi, now destroyed;
18th Dynasty. British Library
(Hay MSS 29822,75).

51

29 Two lutenists. Theban Tomb no.78 of Haremhab; 18th Dynasty.

We are left with just one other banquet ensemble from the tomb of Kynebu, but this is a truly magnificent representation (Fig.30). The painting in this little tomb was destroyed when a huge boulder came crashing down on the roof in the nineteenth century, but fortunately early travellers had previously copied this scene among others in the tomb. The drawings by the artist employed by Robert Hay are particularly useful, reproducing to a high degree of skill and accuracy examples of, as Hay reported, 'careless painting for which we may at the same time conclude the artist was no inferior draughtsman'. The group is performing at the funerary banquet of the tomb owner, an official in the reign of Ramesses VIII, but there is nothing funereal about their appearance: they wear transparent garments and are adorned with garlands, flowers and jewellery. Two girls, not playing instruments, make alluring gestures with their hands. To their right a dark-skinned Nubian girl plays a splendid lyre reminiscent of surviving examples in Berlin decorated with horses' heads; this instrument is symmetrical and has fourteen strings. The girl appears to be plucking the strings with her left hand, but perhaps she originally held a plectrum. The female oboe-player holds one tube of the instrument in the air as if overblowing; the other tube is at a more steeply inclined angle and would have produced the lower note or notes. Joining this merry troupe are two men – members of the priesthood to judge by their garments and shaven heads. One holds his hand to his mouth as if to amplify or alter the sound of his voice; his other hand rests on the shoulder of his companion, a harpist, so it is possible that his eyesight may be impaired. The harp is of the boat-shaped type characteristic of the 18th Dynasty, but it is rather bigger, comparable in size to the famous harps of Ramesses III (see chapter 7), and has fourteen strings. Both of the harpists' hands touch the same strings.

The hieroglyphs do not record the words of the song they are so clearly singing, but they identify the girls as daughters of the tomb owner and songstresses of Amun (a rather common title at this period) and the male singer as 'singer of Amun'. The

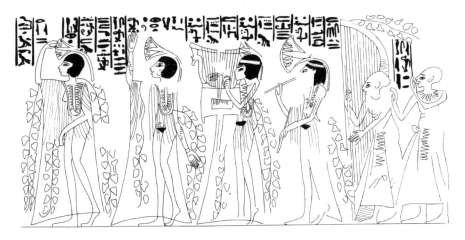

30 Musical ensemble. Theban Tomb no.113 of Kynebu; 20th Dynasty. British Library (Hay MSS 29851,302–3, with some amendments from 29822,122).

text also refers to 'singing to the *ksks*', the dance illustrated in scenes more than a thousand years earlier (p.37).

After the end of the Ramesside Period there are no records of contemporary ensemble music for some six hundred years. The necropolis at Thebes was still used by important officials, but although new elements were introduced into the architecture of the tombs, their decoration was deliberately archaising. The draughtsmen drew strongly on patterns from the past, especially the Old Kingdom, and we are asked to believe that the Egyptians of 600 BC played music of Old Kingdom date. We have to turn to the end of the Pharaonic Period to meet any ensembles comparable to those of earlier dates which reflect the music of the time. A series of reliefs, now in museum collections and possibly all from Memphis, have some interesting novelties to offer (Fig.63).

The conventional Egyptian arched harp has vanished and is replaced by an angular type (see Plate 6). This instrument had been known for some while; in fact, its earliest occurrence is in a banquet ensemble of the mid-18th Dynasty, but this was an isolated case. In the Amarna Period it is shown not infrequently, and the remains of three harps of this type dating from the 19th Dynasty are now in the Cairo Museum. The most splendid example of all is a Late Period harp in the Louvre. Angular harps are usually large, heavy instruments. The sound-box, which can be up to 121cm long, is boat-shaped, made of wood and covered with a wooden board or leather membrane with sound-holes. The neck of surviving instruments is set at a right angle to the sound-box. The suspension rod would rest on transverse bars of wood in the cavity of the sound-box, the strings piercing the leather covering. Marks on surviving instruments suggest that there could be seventeen, nineteen or twenty-one strings. At the upper end they were attached to pegs, which on fine instruments could be made alternately from ebony and ivory.

This type of harp was played with the sound-box held in a vertical position. From an acoustic point of view the difference between the arched harp and the angular harp would have been minimal, but an angular harp would have been able to obtain an even wider range of notes than any of the arched types, even in the unlikely event

53

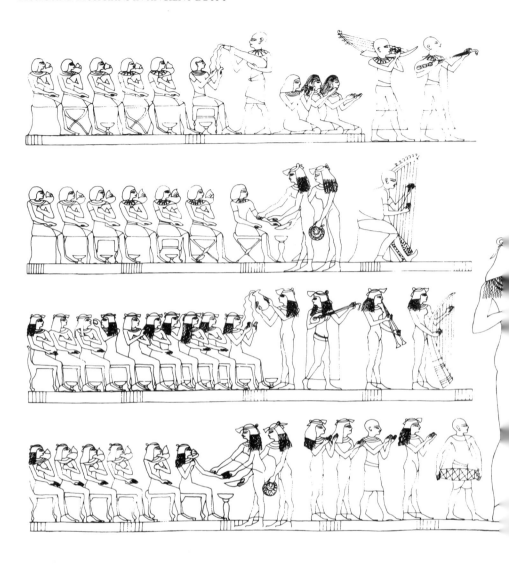

that the strings should be of identical thickness and tension. On such instruments it would be easier for the musician to achieve a progressive scale, if this were indeed his aim.

By the Late Period the form of the lute had developed into the pear-shaped body which may already have been anticipated by the end of the 18th Dynasty (see p.52), with a shorter neck. Two lutes of this type in Berlin are 35cm and 48.5cm long. The smaller of the instruments had two strings, and the larger had three, but one representation suggests that four strings were also possible. The lyre has also changed its appearance; its arms have lost their curve and the instrument almost adopts the rectangular outline of the first lyre seen in Egypt during the Middle Kingdom (pp.37–8).

Rhythm may be provided by women clapping their hands, but in one case we find a woman playing a barrel-shaped drum. In Egypt such drums had been the prerogative of military persons, especially Nubians, and though we find them on rare

31 A banquet scene; 18th Dynasty. Copied by Duemichen (*Historische Inschriften* II, pl.XLB).

occasions in other contexts, they are never played by women. Such instruments usually had a wooden body, with two membranes laced into position (see Plate 3). The drum was suspended from the player's neck and beaten with the hands.

If the drum in this scene can be regarded as a successor to the rectangular tambourine, the ensemble here shows, in its balance of instruments, remarkable similarities with those of earlier date. Only the oboe, or indeed any wind instrument, is missing. A glance at a little-known representation offers an interesting comparison. We know neither the name of the tomb owner nor the location of the tomb (though there can be little doubt that it lay somewhere in the Theban necropolis). The wall decoration was obviously in a perfect state of preservation when it was drawn by the German Egyptologist J. Duemichen (1833–94). Although Duemichen later added embellishments to the scene, these should not distract us. The tomb from which the scene was copied belonged to an official of the 18th Dynasty; the presence of a portable boat-shaped harp in the upper register narrows it down to the mid-18th Dynasty.

The tomb owner and his wife receive the ministrations of the person who is elsewhere often labelled his 'eldest daughter', while male and female guests are lined up on fine chairs placed on mats in the hall or courtyard. Servants pour lavish quantities of fragrant oil on their arms and bring spare necklaces. The musicians are dispersed over four registers, but presumably they are all meant to be in the same room, though perhaps not all playing at the same time: in the upper register men play the portable harp and lute; below is a male harpist; next three girls play the well-known trio of lute, oboe and harp; the scene concludes with a drummer and four people clapping. The presence of the drum is unusual, although one other contemporary tomb (that of a certain Dhout) shows drum with lute and three persons clapping. And, as we have just seen, it was evidently the custom to include a large drum in the ensembles of the Late Period.

It is immensely frustrating not to know more about this tomb-painting, but it must have been one of the grandest banquet scenes in the necropolis, a worthy illustration of a popular song that went:

> Have pleasure in the sight of good cheer, music, dance and song,
> rejoicing with gladness of heart ...[11]

4
Music for the gods

Certain members of the Egyptian pantheon had a particular affinity with music. On a rather intellectual level, a goddess called Merit was considered to be the personification of music, although she never became a goddess of the people with cult chapels of her own. It says something about the Egyptians' desire to express their music visually that she was a 'chironomist goddess', whose major task was to establish cosmic order by means of her song and gestures.

According to Diodorus, Thoth (whom he calls by the Greek name of Hermes) was the first 'to observe the orderly arrangement of the stars and the harmony of the musical sounds and their nature ... He also made a lyre and gave it three strings, imitating the seasons of the year; for he adopted three tones, a high, a low and a medium; the high from the summer, the low from the winter, and the medium from the spring'.[12] Writing and magic were Thoth's domain, and it is not surprising that he should be associated with the role of music in the cosmos. Diodorus wrote in the first century BC, and it must remain an open question as to what extent his reference to the seasons reflects his own background. The lyre played in Egypt had more than three strings. The quotation from Diodorus suggests a basic tuning with substantial intervals, unlike the close intervals, perhaps chromatic, which the evidence would otherwise seem to indicate. The lyre was a late arrival in Egyptian music. So was the oboe, which came in pairs. But according to Juba II, King of Mauretania (c. 25 BC-AD 24), an author of historical works in the Greek language, Osiris was said to have created a 'monaulos', a wind instrument which other writers say was particularly popular in Alexandria.[13] Osiris may well be best known as 'King of the Dead', but he was also 'laughter-loving and fond of music and the dance'.[14]

The only other Egyptian deity who was also a musician was the dwarf god Bes, who was revered as a protector of the home and who assisted at childbirth (see Plate 7). There can be little doubt that ordinary Egyptians felt more at ease with Bes than with any of the principal gods. He was human enough to indulge in secular pastimes, like dancing and playing the drum, tambourine, harp, lyre or oboe. Some of these instruments are being played in his honour on the rare occasion when we see a private (non-royal) individual adoring him face to face, as if he were on a par with the major gods (Fig.72).

Bes played a part on the most intimate occasions in a woman's life – childbirth and even at conception – but it was to Hathor, the 'Golden Goddess', that lovers turned their prayers. Known as the 'mistress of dance' and the 'mistress of music', Hathor seems originally to have been a cow goddess. She is represented either entirely in animal shape or as a woman with cows' ears showing under her wig and, if space permitted, with cows' horns crowning her head. Hathor had many functions. As the celestial cow she was mistress of the sky and gave birth to the sun every morning. She was the daughter of the sun-god Re, and in this capacity she was transformed into a savage lioness greatly feared by men. But she was also assimilated with the more gentle cat goddess, Bastet. As the goddess of love, Hathor was the recipient of votive phalli, and she assisted at divine and royal births. In Thebes she was mistress of the Western Desert, where the dead were buried.

The goddess's many different aspects should not confuse us: it is symptomatic of the Egyptian way of thinking to approach any issue from several angles which were by no means mutually exclusive. Like many other deities, Hathor was versatile and adapted to whichever cloak the theologians put on her shoulders. Towards the end of the Pharaonic Period she frequently lends her attributes to Isis. The role of the latter in ceremonies of rebirth (see below) was a natural progression from the association with Hathor: Isis was the wife of Osiris, King of the Dead, and the mother of Horus whom Osiris engendered posthumously. The trumpet may have played a vital part in the resurrection on a coffin of the Roman Period, for here a female sounds the trumpet to Osiris to the extent that the great god is shedding tears. Although her name is omitted, this can only be Isis.

If few of the gods are depicted playing instruments, there are many representations of temple musicians in paintings and on reliefs. Lone musicians playing directly to a god are depicted largely on private monuments as an act of devotion by the musician himself. In such cases we are often able to establish the name of the performer: a certain Harnakht of Mendes plays a double oboe before the ram-headed god of his town; the harpist Harwoz plays to Haroeris; Zekhensefʿankh plays the harp to Re-Harakhti; the chief singer Raia plays to Ptah. Other representations include a man playing the lyre to Sakhmet; a lutenist named Pedekhons who is represented with his instrument on a statue of the god Khons (see Plate 20); a trumpeter on a statue of the goddess Wazet. The single harpist playing for his god is so common an image that the

32 Bes with a harp. From the temple of Hathor, Philae; Ptolemaic.

33 Painted wooden stela of Zekhensef'ankh; 21st-22nd Dynasty. Louvre (N 3 657).

subject deserves special consideration and a whole chapter is devoted to it (see chapter 7).

An inscription on a statuette of Amenemhab, nicknamed Mahu, refers to his occupation as chief of singers of Amun (see Plate 8). The statuette holds a stela which shows Mahu playing an arched harp to the sun. The text below specifies that the sun is setting on the western horizon, and that Mahu is singing its praises:

> Praise to you millions and millions of times!
> I have come to you, adoring your beauty.
> Your mother Nut [the sky] embraces you.
> You are joyful as you traverse the sky and the earth.
> May the gods of the Underworld worship you [and sing] your praise
> when you hear my words which worship you every day,
> so that you endow me with a burial in peace after enduring old age
> and my *ba* being among my ancestors, following [the king].[15]

Mahu thus played to the sun-god in order to obtain a favour. The deity, shown as the

59

34 Two of the musicians in the temple at Medamud (the remaining follow behind on a wall at right-angles to the one shown here); Ptolemaic.

sun-disc, is named as Re, but Mahu is specifically called 'singer of the noble harp of Amun'. He would have been in office towards the end of the 18th Dynasty, possibly just before the Amarna Period. A second stela of Mahu appeared on the art market in Luxor around 1922, although its present whereabouts is unknown.[16] This stela reported that Mahu 'followed in the king's footsteps in foreign lands', so he must have been a travelling royal harpist. He was even overseer of the singers of the North and South and must thus have been an important person in the musical life of the time. He describes his role as performer in the temple: 'I purify my mouth. I adore the gods. I exalt Horus who is in the sky. I adore him. The Ennead listens, the inhabitants of the Underworld rejoice. They appear at my voice'. He goes on to describe how the gods salute the sun-disc as creator of all; the sentiments expressed on his monument are approaching the religious ideas of Akhenaten.

Numerous instruments already seen in secular contexts are also found in scenes of religious ceremonies and festivals. A little steatite bowl dedicated by a certain Petear-pocrates around 500 BC to the 'Lord of Coptos' has a relief with a row of musicians proceeding towards a shrine containing a large portrait of Hathor (see Plate 9). The musicians form a chain round the bowl, playing a round tambourine, lyre, one-handed clappers and double oboe. One participant slaps her bare buttocks in lieu of an instrument. All of them, judging by their dress, seem to be female (except perhaps for the oboe-player). Unfortunately we cannot tell whether these merry performers were officially attached to the cult of the goddess, or whether they were part of a popular procession.

Another scene showing temple musicians performing in honour of Hathor comes from the Graeco-Roman temple at Medamud, 8km north of Thebes. Three women play the angular harp, a minute barrel-shaped drum and a lute; a fourth woman plays no instrument but appears to be singing. Preceding the whole group are two ladies adorned with flowers; one, who raises her hands, is called 'the one who sweetens evil', a phrase which must surely proclaim the role of music in this particular scene. The caption for the drummer and harpist is unusually eloquent: 'The members of the choir take up their instruments and play them. The songstresses in full number adore the Golden Goddess and make music to the Golden Goddess: they never cease their chanting'. The lutenist and gesticulating lady are accorded the following lines: 'We dance for you; we dance for you, O mistress, the words required by the adorers'. This suggests a mime expressing words in praise of the goddess.

A hymn written behind the lutenist and singer provides further detail about the performance, concluding with universal adoration of the Golden Goddess:

> Come, O Golden Goddess, the singers chant
> (for it is nourishment for the heart to dance the *iba*,
> to shine over the feast at the hour of retiring [?]
> and to enjoy *ḥ*-dance at night).
>
> Come! The procession takes place at the site of drunkenness,
> this area where one wanders in the marshes.
> Its routine is set, the rules firm:
> nothing is left to be desired.
>
> The royal children satisfy you with what you love
> and the officials give offerings to you.
> The lector priest exalts you singing a hymn,
> and the wise men read the rituals.
>
> The priest honours you with his basket,
> and the drummers take their tambourines.
> Ladies rejoice in your honour with garlands
> and girls [do the same] with wreaths.
>
> Drunkards play tambourines for you in the cool night,
> and those they wake up bless you.
> The bedouin dance for you in their garments,
> and Asiatics [dance] with their sticks.
>
> The griffins wrap their wings around you,
> the hares stand on their hind legs for you.
> The hippopotami adore with wide open mouths,
> and their legs salute your face.[17]

We must visualise the musicians, who are representative of a larger group, dancing, playing and singing to the goddess to entertain her and chase away her cares. There seems to be a reference to Hathor in her role as daughter of the sun-god, returning from her rampage in the Southern Desert.

An instrument found frequently in secular scenes of the Old Kingdom but rarely later seems to be appropriate in a religious setting: the end-blown flute. A single flautist is seen in an intimate setting, performing before a god in the presence of a worshipper on a relief (now incomplete), and a pair of male flautists play together at the festival of Sokaris, a funerary deity. The flute, and indeed the oboe, may seem strange choices of instrument for temple musicians, for as wind instruments they could not be used to accompany a hymn sung by the same musician, although they could, of course, have been played during instrumental interludes. The oboe is frequently seen at ritual ceremonies, especially where a priest consecrates an offering to a deceased person: a musician of Hathor may follow the priest, blowing her double pipe. This is reminiscent of the use of the aulos in Greek temples, where offerings were accompanied by this instrument in lieu of the human voice. It is interesting to note in this context, too, that the double oboe was one of the instruments banned from the shrine of Osiris at Philae, but allowed to sound in the neighbouring temple of Hathor (cf. chapter 6).

If all of the instruments mentioned above can be found in secular as well as religious scenes, others have more specific sacred associations, but none more so than the sistrum (from the Greek σείειν, 'to shake'). This was a rattle, but it was also a cult object in its own right, frequently bearing the effigy of Hathor. It came in two forms, the older of which, dating back to the Old Kingdom, is referred to as the 'naos-shaped' sistrum (sššt). This was made from faience and consisted of a straight papyrus-shaped handle with a frame on top in the form of a miniature chapel, or naos; volutes flanking the naos may be a distant reference to Hathor's horns. Within the

35 (*above left*) Musician of Hathor playing an oboe. Theban Tomb no.218 of Amennakht; Ramesside.

36 (*above right*) A fanciful sistrum. Temple at Edfu; Graeco-Roman.

frame were bars of metal with metal discs. As an instrument it would have been perfectly usable, although it would have been fragile and its acoustic properties modest.

The other version is the 'arched' sistrum, or *sḫm* (see Plate 11). It is mentioned in texts as early as the Middle Kingdom, although it is depicted only in the representations from the New Kingdom. This type was made from metal, and had an arched frame instead of a naos. Some instruments were simple, but others had decoration in various forms, most frequently a head of Hathor between the arched frame and the papyrus handle. In the Late Period other elements were added, such as cats and kittens; figures of Bes; uraeus serpents. The oldest sistrum to survive is a votive naos-type instrument dedicated by King Teti (*c.* 234 BC) to Hathor of Dendara, predating by some two thousand years the splendid temple in her honour for which the site is renowned.

Although acoustically the sistrum, especially when made of faience, would have been less impressive than other musical instruments, it may have been precisely this quality which provided its *raison d'être*. From ancient times part of the rite to Hathor had involved pulling up stems of papyrus and shaking them before the goddess, which produced a rattling sound called *sššt*, a most descriptive word which came to designate the naos-shaped sistrum. This ritual was a reminder of the myth of how Hathor took refuge in the papyrus swamps of the Delta with her infant son. Carrying the sistrum was an act of devotion to Hathor, but in addition it came to acquire a more universal significance as a symbol of life and adoration. Thus it can also be seen in contexts which have lost all bearing on the instrument's original function. When Plutarch wrote his treatise on Isis and Osiris in the first or second century AD, the arch of the sistrum was seen as the lunar cycle; the transverse bars were the elements; the twin Hathor head depicted Isis and Nephthys, signifying life and death; the cat was the moon; and the act of wielding this complexity of signs was a symbol of the perpetual movement of all beings. It is little wonder that the sistrum, especially in the Late Period, often carried the name of the king, who would thus be master of all the ideas expressed in it. It is interesting that in the liturgy of the Coptic Church, where the sistrum has survived, the priest extends it to the four cardinal points to emphasise the power of God (see chapter 9).

The sistrum also came to be included in the rites of other gods, and it is often represented in the hands of kings and members of the royal family, or of songstresses of a god. One particularly fine specimen was engraved on its outer surface with a representation of the owner, the 'lady, songstress of Isis, Henuttawy', who is depicted 'shaking the sistrum to your beautiful face, Amun, ruler of Thebes'. Queen Ahmose Nefertari, mother of Amenophis I, was herself worshipped as a goddess; she was known as one 'at the words of whose mouth one rejoices, whose hands are pure when she holds the sistra'. At the other end of the spectrum, we know of a person whose title was 'sistrum-player of Anubis on his mountain'; Anubis was a jackal-god presiding over the embalming house.

The temple songstresses would often perform in groups of three or more, singing a hymn in praise of the god; they probably shook the sistra to divide the phrases of recitation. The sound of the sistrum could be complemented by the rattling of a heavy necklace made of rows of faience beads (*menat*), usually carried by the women in their free hands rather than worn. The necklace included a metal keyhole-shaped element called a counterpoise, which provided a useful handle with which to carry the neck-

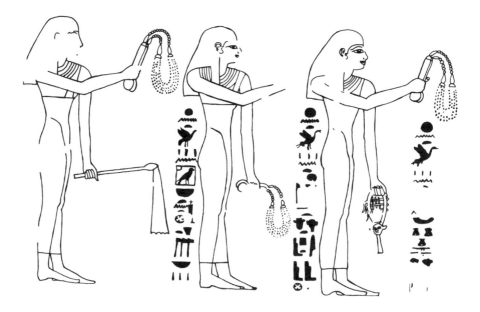

37 Priestesses with sistra and *menats*. Wall-painting in Theban Tomb no.82 of Amenemhet; 18th Dynasty.

lace. The use of the *menat* in such contexts does not in itself turn it into a musical instrument, and *menats* are generally excluded from catalogues of musical instruments.

A wall-painting in the tomb of a certain Amenemhet at Thebes, dating from around 1400 BC, shows three ladies celebrating the Feast of Hathor, which took place on the first day of the fourth month of the inundation season. They are labelled as representatives of the musicians of Amun at Karnak; the musicians of the Great Ennead at Karnak; and the musicians of Hathor at Dendara. The words they chant are written above them: 'I offer to you [Amenemhet] the *menat*, the arched sistrum and the naos-sistrum belonging to Amun, to the Ennead and to Hathor in all her names that they may grant you a fair and long-lasting life'.[18] It is interesting to note that in this representation the musicians are not performing the same movements: no. 1 and no. 3 shake *menats*, whereas no. 2 is shaking a sistrum (now destroyed). No. 1 and no. 2 hold a sistrum and a *menat* respectively, but are not shaking them. The overall effect would seem to have been a combination of mixed rattling sounds. It is, as usual, impossible to tell whether the three musicians perform together or one after another, but since the hymn they chant refers to all three it would seem that in this instance they are indeed making music simultaneously. Another intriguing detail is the curious object held by no. 3 in her left hand. It seems to have no musical function whatever, but perhaps it is related in some way to two other mysterious objects shaped like flywhisks shown in another musical context (see pp.115).

The scene from the tomb of Amenemhet is reminiscent of a passage in the most famous of all Egyptian tales, the story of Sinuhe, written in the 12th Dynasty. Sinuhe, having overheard a plot to murder his king, flees the country. After many hardships, followed by some success abroad, he feels the urge to die in his beloved Egypt. Permission is granted and he returns to the royal palace, where he is introduced to the royal princesses. They wait in the audience hall with their sistra and *menats* and recite a welcoming hymn, undoubtedly rehearsed in advance. It is directed at first to the king; then it turns into a praise of Hathor; finally the singers plead for the ultimate pardon of Sinuhe. During the recital the king's hands touch the sistra and the *menats*. The scene from Amenemhet's tomb gives a lively impression of the rhythmical quality of the performance, but the tale of Sinuhe emphasises their significance as emblems of the goddess, and there is no mention of sound at all. This omission is made up for by Apuleius, the Roman author of *The Golden Ass*. He describes a procession in honour of Isis where those carrying a sistrum shook it three times in succession.[19] We can transcribe this into musical notation as follows:

Another instrument which appears in religious scenes is the round tambourine. It is seen on monuments from Ptolemaic temples, but it has been established that it was already used on religious and ceremonial occasions by the end of the New Kingdom. The earliest representation of it in such a scene is provided by the Theban tomb of Kheruef, dating from the reign of Amenophis III (*c*. 1417–1379 BC), which depicts celebrations for the king's jubilee (see below). It was certainly in popular use by the end of the 18th Dynasty. Remains of round tambourines are rare, but fragments of two parchment membranes, about 40cm in diameter and dating from the end of the New Kingdom, are among the possessions of the Ashmolean Museum in Oxford (see Plate 12). The better preserved of them has an interesting decoration in four horizontal registers showing a number of deities and figures playing the tambourine or dancing with them.

These scenes are closely related to ideas connected with birth: the figures of Isis and Hathor; the dancing girls who may be impersonating Bes; even an anonymous figure who may be a midwife. A set of tambourine membranes now in the Cairo Museum shows similar features, although the instrument to which they belonged was dedicated entirely to Isis; the Cairo membranes are of Ptolemaic date, roughly contemporary with most of the representations of tambourine-playing women on the monuments.

As mentioned above, Hathor was concerned with birth and rebirth, especially in association with Isis. In the Graeco-Roman period the divine birth of the king was celebrated in a special birth-house, referred to in the literature as *mammisi*, a Coptic word meaning literally 'place of birth', adopted by modern scholars as a term for the birth-house. This building was a small temple with a sanctuary surrounded by a portico. Dating to the latest phase of Egyptian civilisation, birth-houses have often survived well. The best can be seen at Philae and Edfu, and at Dendara, which boasts two *mammisi*. The birth of the king, who was identified with the appropriate resident god, was celebrated with music, above all with the beating of tambourines. This was such an impressive occasion that the same kind of music penetrated into other buildings within the temple enclosure, and numerous tambourine-players greet us from the walls. In the largest group of players, at Dendara, no fewer than twenty-nine identical ladies line up, clad in the costume of the goddess herself with cows' horns and sun-disc, beating their instruments in celebration.

In the Roman *mammisi* the tambourine-players are joined by females playing a

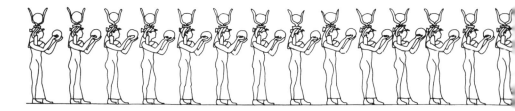

38 Tambourine-players. Temple at Dendara; Ptolemaic.

type of harp not previously seen: a small crescent-shaped instrument resting on a stool (see Plate 13). Such harps are characteristic of the Graeco-Roman Period, played by a temple musician, a queen or the goddess Merit. The crescent-shaped harp was decorated with either a royal head or that of a female with disc and horns, and it had an unusually shallow sound-box. We have an opportunity of studying the instrument in some detail for a model has survived and is now in the collections of the Oriental Institute of Chicago. At just under 40cm tall, it is smaller than most harps seen in the representations. The tip of the neck has broken off, but it is the end of the sound-box which has the decoration – a royal head wearing a double crown and royal head-cloth. The harp's wooden sound-box was solid, so that its dynamic capabilities would have been rather modest. Thirteen holes at the right-hand side of the body would suggest the same number of strings, but the neck has only six holes. This arrangement could be a provision for adjusting the tuning of the instrument. The steep vertical rise of the arch gives quite a large variation in length between the longest and shortest strings available, so with a choice of six out of a possible thirteen stringing positions, the player would have a considerable range of basic notes at her disposal. The final scale would depend on the tension of the strings. Judging by the representations, this type of harp generally had nine strings, but it is unlikely that the Chicago harp could have had more than six. Another string attached to the portion now broken off would have touched the crown of the ornamental figure which would have interfered with the sound.

The line drawing (Fig.39) reconstructs two possible stringing arrangements (a) and (b), showing the positions of the outermost strings in each case. As it would be unthinkable for the harp strings to be other than parallel, the stringing must have been along the lines shown here. The greatest difference in length between the upper and lower string would be obtained in the position marked (b), where the strings are closest to the neck, with a ratio of 2:3. This would have given the strings an approximate range of an augmented fifth. It may be mentioned that in representations of two arched harps in the temple of Sethos I at Abydos the strings have been drawn almost identically to this reconstruction. It has generally been assumed that the design had been emended by the draughtsman, but the strings may have been drawn double intentionally to show alternative arrangements.

The crescent-shaped harp was not only played in the *mammisi*, but also accompanied hymns to other gods, punctuating the chant as shown for example in the temple of Mut at Karnak. In this case the harpist is followed by a tambourine-player, both following in the footsteps of King Ptolemy II, who presents sistra to Mut and to the lion goddess Sakhmet, worshipped in the same locality.

In the later phases of Pharaonic civilisation other instruments were also used for ritual purposes. A rhyton (horn) is not an instrument generally associated with Egypt. In the reign of Akhenaten forty 'horns' were sent as a gift from Tushratta, King of Mitanni (see chapter 6). Over a thousand years later Athenaeus, a Greek writer based in Egypt in the third century AD, describes the use of the rhyton in a temple of Arsinoë in the Delta. Athenaeus quotes an epigram by the poet Hedylos mentioning the rhyton made by the engineer Ctesibius:

> Come hither, ye drinkers of strong wine, look also at this rhyton in the temple of Arsinoë the Gracious . . . it is in the form of the Egyptian Besas, the dancer who trumpets forth a shrill noise when the spout is opened for the flowing wine – no signal for battle is this, but through the golden mouthpiece there rings the signal for revelling and mirth. It is like the ancestral melody which the Lord Nile produced from the divine waters, dear to the initiates who bring him their offerings. Nay then, if ye will know this clever device of Ctesibius, come hither young men, beside the temple of Arsinoë here.[20]

Although this was a period of strong Greek influence, especially in the Delta, the combination of drinking and devotion typical of the cult of Hathor can still be recognised.

The cymbals shared with the rhyton the triple purpose of drinking vessel, musical instrument and ritual object (see Plate 10). A cymbal has survived bearing the inscription: 'To the Great Goddess', the deity no doubt being Cybele. A pair of cymbals, now in the British Museum, was found with the mummy of a certain Ankh-hap, who was door-keeper in the temple of Amun, probably in the first century AD. It would be interesting to know if they really belonged to Ankh-hap and, if so, whether he played his cymbals in the course of his duties in the temple. The use of cymbals is referred to by Clement of Alexandria (c. AD 150–211/16), who says that libations were offered to Cybele in cymbals.[21] At a feast of Isis a eunuch called Zenobius was hired to play cymbals during a dance; he was also proficient with the tambourine and crotals (a pair of small cymbals attached to a hinged U-shaped handle). Hathor, who at this time often borrowed attributes and rites from both Isis and Cybele, likewise appreciated these instruments, according to an inscription in the temple at Dendara: after the harvest the statue of Hathor was carried out of the temple and presented to the people to the sound of cymbals and tambourines. It is easy to imagine that this was cause for jubilation and an invitation to dancing. These references are all of fairly late date, but the use of cymbals is firmly rooted in Pharaonic civilisation; they

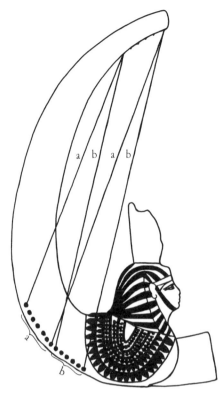

39 Crescent-shaped harp, showing the possibilities of suspending the strings.

are mentioned in texts dating from the Middle Kingdom, but in this case they are played by goddesses – Isis and her sister Nephthys – rather than by temple musicians.

The Egyptians' preoccupation – almost obsession – with the ideas of birth and rebirth was a fundamental element of their funerary beliefs: rebirth was one of the stages of existence in the afterlife. The ceremonies that took place in the *mammisi* were part of the official cults closely associated with the divine person of the ruler. Ordinary people would have had little opportunity to participate in these rituals, and there is scant evidence for popular versions of such birthing ceremonies which may have involved music. The only clue in this direction is the role of the dwarf god Bes, protector of women in childbirth, who was often portrayed as a musician (see above). Other official ceremonies connected with rebirth may have involved the populace to some extent. One of these was the *sed*-festival, which marked the thirtieth year of the king's reign. It originated in the ancient custom whereby the king was obliged to prove his physical capabilities every thirty years in a ceremony called *heb sed*. From the Old Kingdom the most memorable jubilee was that celebrated by King Zoser. The enclosure which incorporates his magnificent step pyramid at Saqqara included a number of buildings planned for the celebration of Zoser's jubilee in his afterlife.

It is a peculiar fact that this feast, which must have been a major event in the reign of any pharaoh who ruled for thirty years or more, is highlighted in the monuments of very few reigns. Just a handful of the recorded *sed*-jubilees are significant for our purposes in establishing the role of music on these occasions: those of Amenophis III and

IV and of Osorkon III (883–855 BC). The jubilee of Amenophis III is best commemorated in the tomb of Kheruef, one of his officials. The wall-decoration of the tomb, at Thebes, was sculpted in immaculate low relief, and has survived well because it was sanded over at an early date. The tomb robbers who eventually desecrated the monument failed to discover the scenes which interest us, showing the jubilee. The singers and musicians can be seen on the two walls on either side of the entrance to the inner room in a prominent and well-lit position. On the right Amenophis III and his queen are present at the ceremony of 'raising the <u>dd</u>-pillar'; this object was a symbol of the stability of the rule, erected on the night before the jubilee. While the pillar is hauled into an upright position, groups of men and women take part in a sacred performance consisting of dance and mock fighting, the recital of hymns and the sound of rhythm. 'Women from the oases' dance, raising their arms above their heads. They are preceded by two women with tambourines and six others clapping their hands while the pillar is raised. In front of the pillar ten men dance, each raising one arm and a foot, while on either side three and four men respectively clap their hands and recite a hymn. Dancers impersonating the mythological 'people of Dep and Pe' (souls of ancient kings) recreate a ritual battle armed with stems of papyrus, the outcome determining the right of Horus to succeed his father Osiris.

The ritual performance continues on the opposite side of the doorway. The royal couple is leaving the palace accompanied by priests and princesses. Below, a different pantomime is taking place: fifteen young girls perform a series of athletic movements. Two pairs make two symmetrical movements, lifting one arm and raising the other from hip level to touch the elbow. The poses of the remaining participants, however, suggest gymnastics rather than dance. It is impossible to tell whether the fifteen girls are performing the steps simultaneously, or whether two or three pairs are shown at different stages of the performance: considering the generally narrative quality of Egyptian representation the latter would seem more likely. In the register below are more pairs of girls in three virtually symmetrical poses; each pair kneels in a different position making movements with the arms: clearly they seek to convey a message – if only we knew what it is! The scene continues with four squatting women who are clapping their hands, two who are lifting one foot and appear to move towards a group of squatting musicians, and four who gesture with their hands. The four clapping women may also be singing or humming a tune, if our interpretation of the hieroglyphs written above their heads is correct (see the Introduction). At the opposite end of the register is a procession consisting of a tambourine-player, six women clapping their hands, three dancers wearing Old Kingdom hairstyles, a priest concealed behind an animal mask, and two corpulent men dancing. With just a few exceptions, the performers are female.

The group of squatting musicians is an ensemble of three female flautists and a singer. As we have seen above, the flute does appear in religious scenes in the New Kingdom and later, but an ensemble of flautists at this date is unusual. The flute must have remained in popular use, for it has survived to this day as the *nây*, but it ceased to be depicted in banquet ensembles after the Middle Kingdom. This is surprising, as few instruments produce a more alluring and agreeable sound than the *nây*. The songstress in our group is equally archaic: she performs the gestures of a chironomist, apparently defunct in Egyptian representations at this time. It is possible that the art of chironomy had been kept alive and was in more general use than the evidence suggests, but it could also be that the scene is a copy or a reinterpretation of a motif from earlier times, used to emphasise the traditional aspect of this occasion.

Like some of his predecessors, Amenophis III decided to repeat his *sed*-jubilee a few years later, and he appears to have been in the midst of preparations for his fourth jubilee when he died. His son Akhenaten, who broke with tradition in many ways (see chapter 6), turned the occasion into a jubilee for his god, the Aten or sun-disc, at the beginning of his reign. There are numerous scenes from his chapels at Karnak which show the king in his short, tight-fitting jubilee garment under the rays of the sun: god and king celebrating together. The artists would have had their motifs fresh in their minds, for the decoration in the tomb of Kheruef was hardly completed when the new ruler came to the throne. Some of the scenes connected with the feast appear to have been omitted, but among the tens of thousands of decorated blocks from the buildings of Akhenaten reused as core material by subsequent rulers we find representations of gymnastic dances identical to those in Kheruef's tomb.

When we turn to the much later scenes on the walls of the Festival Hall of Osorkon III at Bubastis, we find that some things had changed. Unfortunately only about one third of the decoration has survived, but we have one female flautist; three pairs of kneeling dancers whose arms are in slightly different positions; a row of women, one of whom beats a large tambourine and whose companions raise their arms instead of clapping their hands. In addition there are groups of priests, including one who balances a tambourine so large that a second priest behind him has to help keep it steady.

If the jubilee celebrations offered only limited participation for the people, other religious festivals were truly popular. The best evidence for such occasions comes from representations of the Opet Feast and the Feast of the Valley. In the great processions military and sacred music combined to create a festive atmosphere. The Opet Feast celebrated the 2km journey of Amun from his habitual residence in the temple of Karnak to the temple of Luxor and back again. The statue of the god travelled partly on land, carried in a model boat on the shoulders of the priests, and partly in a real boat on the river, while crowds of spectators gathered on the banks. Scenes from an Opet Feast celebrated in the reign of Tutankhamun decorate the walls of a colonnade in the Luxor temple and give a lively impression of the splendour of the occasion. Soldiers were present not only to control the proceedings but also to entertain. Drummers played: a Nubian drummer wearing jingles around his ankles holds his drum at an angle, while an Egyptian drummer has his in a steady horizontal position. Trumpeters blow their instruments: one man holds his trumpet up towards the sky in an effort to make himself heard. Groups of Libyans, recognisable by their feathered head-dresses, beat their clappers, perhaps to keep people on the move, perhaps to beat a tattoo. In one scene there are priestesses with their sistra, and joining the party are three lutenists who would undoubtedly have played predominantly rhythmic figures, more in keeping with the occasion than melodic lines. Although some lutes had frets, the subtleties of subdividing the strings and playing a melody would have been lost on an occasion like the Feast of Opet, with all the noise, shouting and rejoicing on the river. The lutenists are named as singers from the town of Kheshyt; their mouths are firmly closed and corners of their mouths are turned down – their flaring nostrils suggest they are humming. Female gymnasts have turned out in force, showing off with somersaults, their long hair streaming out through the air and their backs arching. A loin cloth was deemed the proper garment for these girls, allowing them to display the full beauty of their bodies in motion. The sense of movement and jostling of the crowds confined in a narrow space is typical of the style of the Amarna Period, of which the reign of Tutankhamun was the closing phase.

Queen Hatshepsut also commemorated this event in her so-called 'Red Chapel' at the temple of Amun at Karnak. Selected scenes carved on the red quartzite blocks survive, but, like Akhenaten's monuments, the building had been dismantled during antiquity and the stones reused in the foundations of other buildings. As many blocks carry complete scenes, the task of matching and assembling them is not an easy one. Two blocks bear representations of which the details are similar, although their arrangement varies. Each shows three ladies with sistra; a man playing an arched harp with a short hymn to Amun; a group of gymnasts executing somersaults; three men clapping their hands above their heads; and, on one block, two male dancers. A caption reads: 'How sweet is the scent of the temple of Amun . . . The god is coming for his journey' – a description of the proceedings to be chanted or recited to ensure that the scenes represented on the monument would continue in perpetuity.

The Feast of the Valley was an equally grand occasion, but we can gain glimpses of it only by piecing together information from a number of different temples and private monuments. This feast again celebrated a journey undertaken by Amun of Karnak, this time across the river to the west bank, where the tombs and royal mortuary temples had been constructed. The goal was the temple built by Queen Hatshepsut under the steep cliffs of Deir el-Bahari. The procession's route was lined with people who had gathered while visiting the tombs of their relatives; indeed, the dead themselves were believed to come out and enjoy the spectacle. The relatives brought them flowers, the 'bouquet of Amun'; sistra and *menats* were shaken as a token of Hathor. Priestesses, male singers and gymnasts were depicted in various combinations on the walls of some tombs in the area. A private individual such as Menkheperresonb, first prophet of Amun in the reign of Tuthmosis III, had three songstresses represented in his tomb, singing a song which included a praise to the king:

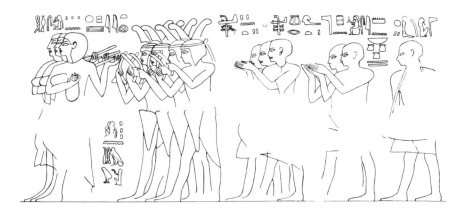

40 Musicians in the procession of the Feast of Opet. Luxor Temple; end of the 18th Dynasty.

41 The Feast of Opet. Relief from a building erected by Queen Hatshepsut; 18th Dynasty.

> To your *ka*! The sistra and *menats* of Amun, when the god takes his seat on the great throne of the West [at Deir el-Bahari] in great joy. You follow your king with a glad heart and chant to his fair face. You worship the goddess who is on his forehead [the uraeus-serpent] while myriads are around him, that he may give rejuvenating breath to your nostril when you come from the temple after performing acceptable rites.[22]

Again, the chant not only explains the action, but also, with the assistance of the rattling instruments, enhances its effect. The tomb owner liked to envisage the temple singers actually coming to the door of his tomb and reciting phrases, which would include his name and would express such pious wishes as: 'Receive [the sistra and *menats*] presented to your nostril, you who are of the millions near [the god], and may he give fresh breath to your nostrils every day'.

Alongside these grand feasts, the Egyptian calendar was studded with local festivals. We are particularly well informed about those celebrated at Thebes, which was the religious centre for about a thousand years. Among them was a feast of the fertility god Min commemorated on the walls of the mortuary temple of Ramesses III; as well as the usual military music provided by drums and trumpets, the flute was blown and Libyans played the two-handed clappers. Other scenes show musicians performing during the festivals of particular gods: in the tomb of Nakhtamun, head of the altar in the mortuary temple of Ramesses II, the performers include the singer of the Ramesseum, Nesune; the singer of Ptah-Sokar, Neferaha; and two anonymous musicians, one playing a splendid lute, the other clapping his hands. They are all shown with parted lips, chanting a short prayer to Ptah-Sokar-Osiris and imploring the god to protect the king. Such scenes must have taken place on innumerable occasions in all the major temples in Egypt.

Another official who was head of the altar towards the end of the Ramesside Period was Imiseba, who is also shown in an intimate offering scene. His tomb at Thebes illustrated a feast in honour of the 'Theban Triad' – Amun, Mut and Khons.

The divine images are carried in procession in sacred boats, accompanied by a drummer. When the images arrive at their goal three musicians - a harpist, a lutenist and a singer – assist the priests, who make offerings on behalf of the king. Above are written the words of their chant, each phrase being introduced by the word 'Awake!', addressed to Amun-Re. This pattern was no doubt reflected in the accompanying music.

The picture we can form of Egyptian sacred music and its significance for the population at large is complex. Although the period covered is vast – some three thousand years – religion must have been the most conventional aspect of Egyptian civilisation. The most obvious visual symbol of its conservatism is the Egyptian temple; its spiritual backbone is the liturgy, a large part of which consisted of reliving ancient myths. From the available evidence the tradition of liturgical music was less prominent than that concerned with dramatic texts, but we are frustrated in our search for clues and have to confine ourselves to secondary sources – those occasions which the visual artists chose to commemorate. Literary references to music are few and far between, and any specialist treatises on the subject have yet to be discovered. We must content ourselves with stray references to musical performance, such as one in a hymn to Amun-Re, mentioning not only that 'men sing to him in every chapel', but also that 'his is the singing in the night when it is dark'. These enigmatic comments and the following text seem to refer to one of the god's festivals, when beer was drunk and people sang of him on the rooftops. Here we are reminded of the banquet scenes, and once again the intimate links between the sacred and secular in ancient Egyptian society are confirmed.

5
Military and processional music

In its narrowest sense the military music of the Egyptians is easy to define, for the instruments are few and their melodic capacity limited. Hence we are forced to conclude that excellence was judged on rhythmical performance, and perhaps on secondary factors such as the stamina of the player and the strength of his instrument. There is evidence to suggest that the occupation of a military musician was a highly skilled one.

The archetypal military instruments were the barrel-shaped drum and the trumpet, and it is in the New Kingdom, in the reign of Queen Hatshepsut, that we meet them in representations of the sovereign's men. The drum, however, appears to have been known even earlier, for a well-preserved instrument, now in the Cairo Museum, was found next to a coffin in a Middle Kingdom tomb at Beni Hassan. It is about 65cm long with a width of about 29cm at either end. This instrument was made by hollowing out a section of palm trunk, so that the barrel shape is less pronounced than in later drums. Fragments of the leather membranes and lacing survive, and since the latter prevented the wood from fading, the exact pattern of the lacing is imprinted on the body of the drum. A coil of leather found with the drum but now apparently lost suggested to the excavators that the membranes could have been tuned by inserting the coil into the lacings and twisting it with a stick.

A further four drums of this type have survived but they are of a much later date, although one, also in Cairo, has been tentatively dated to the 18th Dynasty from the appearance of the palmette decoration on the loops used to suspend the drum around the player's neck. The body of this drum is made of bronze, an unusual if not unique material for an Egyptian drum. Its dimensions are similar to those of the Beni Hassan drum, but the barrel shape is clearly marked. A drum in the Louvre, and another in the Metropolitan Museum of Art in New York, are both of a different construction. The Louvre's drum is in a near-perfect state of preservation (see Plate 3). Radiography has revealed that its body is made of twenty-four boards glued together; the boards are wider in the middle, giving the instrument a true barrel shape. Two red membranes were connected by an intricate system of parallel lacing.

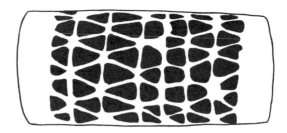

42 Barrel-shaped drum; Middle Kingdom(?). Egyptian Museum, Cairo (CG 69354).

The lacing of the drum in New York is in a less perfect condition, but otherwise similar.

The ancient Egyptians usually called this drum *kmkm*, aptly describing its sound. They did not use barrels for any other purpose, and since the preferred shape was not dictated by the material itself (the palm trunk is the exception), it must have been determined by convention and a recognition of its inherent acoustic properties: the sound produced by a barrel-shape must have been considered more satisfactory than that of a cylinder. All the instruments in the representations are clearly barrel shaped and not cylindrical.

Not surprisingly, it required certain skills to play this deceptively simple instrument, and anyone wishing to become a drummer in the army had to pass a test. This has recently been revealed by a new study of a text of the late 17th Dynasty, predating any of the known representations of this drum. A certain Emhab had been practising his drum secretly, keeping his fingers strong and supple to extract a variety of sounds from his instrument (sticks were never used for this purpose). Then one day he was invited to an audition to try his skills against those of another contestant. Emhab beat his rival by performing no fewer than seven thousand 'lengths'. The nature of such a 'length' is not explained, but this must be a technical term, perhaps describing a 'figure' or a rhythmical phrase. Having gained the position as army drummer, Emhab spent a whole year drumming every single day, following his king (Kamose?) on his campaigns and bravely executing every command until, finally, he was rewarded with a female slave, purchased for him by the king himself. Many of the drummers in the representations are Nubians, and their efforts could inspire their companions to jump up and dance, showing that there was room for improvisation among the rank and file on special occasions. The barrel-shaped drum itself may well have been introduced to Egypt from the south.

The trumpet (*šnb*) appeared in representations at the same time as the drum, in reliefs in the temple of Hatshepsut at Deir el-Bahari. However, no instruments survive from before the New Kingdom; in fact, our only two examples were among the objects deposited in the tomb of Tutankhamun (see Plate 14). Earlier literature occasionally refers to a third trumpet in the Louvre, but this object has now been demonstrated not to be a musical instrument at all, but the lower part of a stand or incense-burner. This may also be the case with an inscribed 'trumpet' found by W.M.F. Petrie at Thebes. Unfortunately the object was stolen from the excavations and the matter cannot be investigated.

The instruments shown on the monuments appear to be of two shapes: one a slender instrument in which the tube gradually splays out into the bell; the other with a marked transition from the still slightly conical tube to a shorter and more flaring bell. Interestingly, the two instruments of Tutankhamun represent both varieties. The ends which were blown are identical; for a more comfortable contact with the lips the tube was inserted into a metal sleeve, the upper edge of which was provided with a ring. There is no evidence of any other mouthpiece having been used.

One of Tutankhamun's trumpets is a slender instrument made of beaten silver with a golden 'mouthpiece' and a decorative golden band at the bell. The tube and bell were made separately and soldered together, but the general impression is of a uniform shape. The other trumpet is made of copper or bronze with gold overlay at either end of the tube, leaving a section in the middle the colour of black ebony. The

43 Trumpeter. Temple of Ramesses II at Abydos; 19th Dynasty.

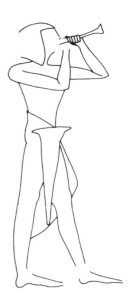

'mouthpiece' is made of silver. The trumpets are, respectively, 58.2cm (silver) and 49.4cm (copper) long; the diameters of their upper ends are 1.7 and 1.3cm, and the maximum diameters of the bells are 8.2 and 8.4cm. Both are decorated with a square panel on the bell, showing Amun, Re-Harakhti and Ptah and, on the copper trumpet, the king himself. The silver trumpet originally had a design of a lotus flower, admirably suited to its shape, but this was partly erased to make room for the panel. It was also inscribed with the king's cartouches, placed so as to be seen by the person blowing the instrument. The insertion of the panel, to be seen from the opposite end, rather mars the appearance of this otherwise elegant object.

The trumpets of Tutankhamun are the only instruments which have been made to produce an authentic ancient Egyptian sound. A record of the experiments has been reproduced by a number of scholars, including myself, largely based on the account given by H. Hickmann in his monograph on the trumpets and a report in *The Listener* of 1946, when the sound was first broadcast. It is thus recorded that the trumpets were played in 1939 with modern mouthpieces inserted, and in 1941 without any gadgets applied. Hickmann was present at the second attempt and records that the notes obtained for the copper trumpet were (1) a note between C and C# and (2) a note close to E♭ in the register above. A replica of the silver trumpet was blown, the original having apparently been damaged during the previous attempt. The replica, being for some reason 7mm shorter than the original, produced (1) a note between A and B♭ and (2) a note slightly lower than C in the register above (the notes of the original being slightly lower).

The alleged first attempt, using modern mouthpieces, was carried out by a bandsman Tappern. What is less well known is that the trumpets had indeed been blown as early as 1933 by Percival Robson Kirby, later Head of the Department of Music at the University of Witwatersand, Johannesburg. In his autobiography he gives a vivid account of his experience (I am indebted to Professor Kirby's nephew, A.J.K. Monro BSc DPE, for supplying me with this reference):

I left England on 25 January [1933] ... Armed with a letter of introduction to

Dr. Engelbach, Keeper of the Royal Egyptian Museum, I visited that establishment and began a systematic search for ancient Egyptian musical instruments ... he [Dr Engelbach] got quite excited, and took me to see the marvellous relics that had been found in the tomb of TutAnkhAmen. As soon as I saw the two trumpets, one of bronze and the other of silver, I said to him that I was sure that they could be sounded, as they were in such perfect condition. On this he told me that if I would come to his office next morning he would have the instruments ready for me to try. This I did, and, finding that each of the two trumpets contained a core of wood, obviously kept there to preserve them from being accidentally dented when not in use, I removed these, and, taking up each instrument in turn, blew a resounding blast on it. There were, of course, no mouthpieces of the kind we use today on brass instruments, but the mouth ends of the tubes were turned over a ring of wire, this forming an *embouchure* by means of which it was quite easy to produce a ringing sound from the instruments. But only one effective note could be elicited from each trumpet, though a single, though ineffective, lower sound could also be produced ... My performance was the very first occasion on which the TutAnkhAmen trumpets were sounded, for the statements sometimes made that Mr. Howard Carter blew them when he discovered them in the tomb is quite untrue, as also was the 'priority claim' made by the BBC when the instruments were sounded by James Tappern, trumpeter of the 'Cherry-pickers', for a broadcast from Cairo six years after my visit to that city. What was infinitely worse was that for the broadcast the military trumpeter, finding as I had done that he could get only one good note out of each instrument, fitted his own modern trumpet mouthpiece into each of the ancient instruments in turn, thus completely altering their nature, and enabling him to blow brilliant fanfares quite alien to the sounds heard by the Egyptian soldiery of antiquity, and thus misleading listeners-in, including one of the leading London music critics.

According to Hickmann a strong pressure of air was required to produce sounds without a modern mouthpiece, and the high notes were especially hard to obtain (thus rather contradicting Kirby's experience). The experiment can easily be tried out on the lower half of an English postal horn: the dimensions are not dissimilar to those of the copper trumpet and it produces a similar set of notes (c^1 and d^2). The recordings made on each of the occasions when the trumpets were blown have been broadcast a number of times and have been included on historical records. The sound of the deeper notes of each instrument is rich and powerful, not unlike that of the Nordic lur (a large, S-shaped trumpet), and, judging by the timbre of other Egyptian wind instruments, exactly to the liking of the Egyptians. A graphic representation of the harmonics registered when the instruments were blown explains better than any words the irregularity and roughness of the oscillations, especially with regard to the replica of the silver trumpet, which was made of very thin sheet metal. The limited number of notes available suggest that rhythm and power were of the essence.

On some of the monuments trumpeters appear to be shown in pairs, although in most cases only one of the players has his instrument to his lips. Pairs of instruments are known from other civilisations, and even from Egypt itself, as for example, a pair of sistra from the tomb of Tutankhamun. The Nordic lur came in pairs, as did Jewish

44 Trumpeter on a fortress. Relief from the mortuary temple of Ramesses III at Medinet Habu; 20th Dynasty.

45 (below) Military Nubian dancers. Tomb no.78 of Haremheb at Thebes; 18th Dynasty.

trumpets, and pairs of trumpets are still played in India and Tibet. The general consensus seems to be that the two members of a pair were played in unison or alternately, with no polyphony intended. The evidence from ancient Egypt is, as we have seen, uncertain, although some representations do seem to show one player holding two instruments. This brings us to a second question, which concerns wooden dummies found inside the Tutankhamun trumpets. In outline they are identical to the trumpets they belonged to, and it may be that they were used during the manufacture of the instruments, when the sheet metal was being beaten. In the case of fragile instruments with thin walls it is quite possible that the cores were kept and inserted into the trumpets to prevent them from being damaged when not in use. The 'second' trumpet in a representation could thus be the core rather than the instrument itself, held by an assistant. In one case, however, the trumpeter is apparently already carrying the core under his arm. The 'bells' of the cores of Tutankhamun's trumpets were coated with a layer of gesso and painted, which would perhaps have rendered them unsuitable for daily use, but it is possible that they were decorated especially for the burial of the king. The use of the core or stopper would mute the instruments and prevent them from giving out unintentional noises to disturb the king. However, alternative interpretations are also possible: the lotus flower which forms the decoration was a powerful symbol of rebirth, and it is difficult not to see some connection with the aspirations for the king's future in this particular choice of ornament. In a much later representation of Roman date a person is shown blowing a trumpet before Osiris, King of the Dead. The scene is painted on a coffin, so the relation to funerary beliefs of the time is thus not in question. The trumpets of Tutankhamun would thus seem to have served a double purpose: in real life as a military instrument, and in the afterlife as an aid to the king's resurrection. The change of decor-

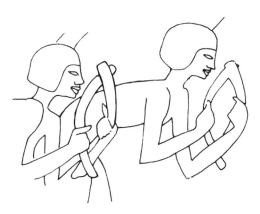 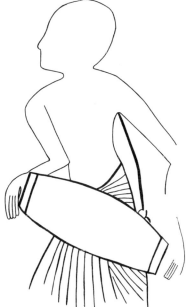

46 (above) Soldiers with two-handed clappers. Block originally from a building of Akhenaten, and reused in the ninth pylon at Karnak; end of the 18th Dynasty.

47 (right) Drummer. Theban Tomb no.65 of Imiseba; 20th Dynasty. British Library (Hay MSS 29851,128).

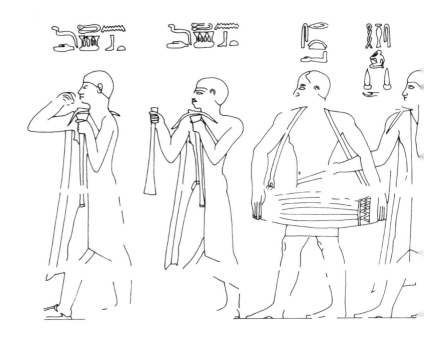

48 Musicians.
Temple at Kawa;
25th Dynasty.

ation in the silver trumpet would seem to emphasise this, although it appears that it was first made as burial equipment (with lotus flower decoration), then adapted to a military purpose (with the insertion of the panel), and finally buried in the tomb.

Drum and trumpet were frequently used together, although they could also be played separately. In representations of military campaigns the drum was omitted, but we must however remember Emhab, the drummer, who allegedly followed his king to war (see above). In the grand battle scenes of Ramesses II and III trumpeters are shown in action blowing from the rooftops of a captured fortress, marshalling a team of horses or a group of armed soldiers, or saluting the king as he sets forth in his chariot. These trumpeters clearly have an important position, for the power of their instrument enabled them to make themselves heard to a large number of people and at some distance. The principal of the megaphone, in which the trumpet found its origin, indicates that this was its primary function, and this is confirmed by an inscription in a temple of the 25th Dynasty at Kawa in Nubia: the hieroglyphs referring to a trumpeter include the verb *dd* (to speak) beside the word for trumpet. The text seems to read 'trumpet speaker', and from the New Kingdom the title *dd m šnb* was used, with the phrase *ʿš m šnb* (caller on the trumpet). Trumpeters must have developed a series of rhythmical signals with which to communicate their message, perhaps in the manner of: 'Move faster!', 'Halt!', 'Turn!', 'Attack!' and so on. A trumpeter in possession of two instruments of different pitch would have found his vocabulary accordingly enriched.

The army and military musicians were also employed for more peaceful pursuits, and where we see soldiers taking part in processions and other public performances we have a much more relaxed picture. Crowds of people would attend on these occasions, and the skills of the trumpeter would be needed to keep the procession under

control and the spectators at bay. This is where the drummer is also in evidence, frequently joined by other performers on rhythmical instruments, such as the two-
handed clappers, or even by soldiers clapping their hands. Queen Hatshepsut was
the first to commemorate such a grand occasion on a wall of her mortuary temple at
Deir el-Bahari. She had sent an expedition to the granite quarries at Aswan south of
Thebes to bring back two great obelisks for her buildings at Karnak. The arrival of
the two monoliths called for celebration, and the army was summoned to receive the
barges as they appeared on the river. Unloading the massive stones would have
required some organisation, and again the trumpeter would have been welcome. The
drummer added a festive touch, and priests and butchers were at hand to consecrate
offerings to Amun, in whose honour the obelisks had been carved.

During the procession of Hathor, mistress of the mountain in whose shadow Hatshepsut's temple was built, the soldiers paraded with their regimental standard and
mascot (a panther) and two Libyans performed a dance with sticks in their hands, accompanied by three colleagues beating boomerang-shaped clappers. The Libyans
are easily recognisable by the feathers in their head-dresses, as well as by the accompanying inscription. They seem to have been especially adept at handling these
clappers, for they are often portrayed in just this situation. Two pairs of clappers of
the type illustrated have been discovered. They are made of wood, 25.6 and 38.5cm
long, with a rounded outer and a flat inner surface.

The musicians of the army of the great warrior king Tuthmosis III are represented
only in the tomb of the vizier Amenuser: a trumpeter, a drummer and a group of men
clapping their hands are part of the military escort accompanying the king as he is
carried to the temple in a palanquin. Thanuny, a commander of soldiers under Tuthmosis IV, was represented in office in his tomb at Thebes: the military parade passing
before his eyes included standard-bearers, a trumpeter and dancing Nubians. A

colleague of his, Haremhab, extended the subject, and in his tomb is a scene showing the bringing of foreign tribute to the king; a festive display of Egyptians and their horses; Syrians with the precious metal vases for which they were famed; and Nubians with gold, ivory and ebony, along with their womenfolk, children and cattle. The group of Nubians included dancers, as well as a trumpeter and a drummer, and these must have been in an unenviable position: not only did they serve in the king's army, but they even had to take their fellow countrymen to him as slaves.

During the Amarna Period the basic picture of military music remains much the same, but we are presented with additional details which make this short span of years so fascinating. In one scene Libyans with their clappers accompany an improvised dance in the street, with people jumping in the air, twisting and turning in spite of their richly pleated kilts. In contrast, in the scenes from the king's early years at Karnak military musicians are surprisingly rare. The trumpet is shown once (out of context), and the large drum occurs in a different setting altogether. On the other hand, two blocks depict Libyans with their boomerang-shaped clappers, undoubtedly rousing the inhabitants of Thebes during a royal procession.

The most splendid celebrations recorded by a king must be the Opet Feast of Tutankhamun which is commemorated on the walls of the Luxor temple (see chapter 4). Here military and sacred musical performances are combined with gymnastic displays and dancing in what must have been a truly colourful popular event. The Ramesside kings employed their military musicians for similar purposes. Ramesses II left a large-scale representation in the courtyard of his temple at Abydos showing a procession of offering-bringers with decorated fat bulls, flowers and a gazelle, soldiers, fan-bearers, charioteers and a trumpeter. A drummer, hand-clapping men and a group of Libyans with very small clappers form the receiving committee. A Nubian carries his drum round his neck, but he is not actually playing it: the stick he holds in one hand would have been too long to be practical for that purpose, and drumsticks are not otherwise known.

In the temple of Armant in Upper Egypt, probably contemporary with the Abydos temple, we meet not one but two Nubian drummers as well as a dancer in a hunting procession. Again, the way in which the Nubians hold their drums is unusual and they are possibly performing dance steps at the same time as drumming. The festival of Min which took place in the reign of Ramesses III has already been referred to (see chapter 4). Once more the drum and trumpet are played by Libyans with feathered head-dresses. This drum is a peculiar shape, the membranes being smaller than the player's hands. Another episode from the same festival shows the trumpeter facing the drummer; he appears to be holding two trumpets up with their bells downwards, but the scene is partly destroyed, so we cannot be sure what is happening. If it were not for the context one might suggest that the objects are not actually trumpets but incense-burners.

This intriguing scene provides a link with another dating from the last phases of Pharaonic civilisation. When the Nubian kings of the 25th Dynasty seized power, instead of imposing their own native culture they adopted the trappings of Egyptian civilisation, and brought its conventions to their home far to the south. The temple of Kawa near modern Dongola (Sudan) was dedicated to Amun, although the locality was curiously named Gem-pa-aten – 'Aten (sun-disc) is found'. If this was inspired by the ill-fated temple of the Aten at Karnak which bore the same name, it shows that not all records of the Amarna Period had been destroyed, as is generally assumed. The walls of the temple are decorated in true Egyptian style, and their subject matter is just as authentic. Two scenes depict offering-bringers and musicians with instruments which, with the exception of the two large angular harps, were known from military processions: the drum and the trumpet. The trumpets are carried by the players rather than being blown, reminiscent of the way in which the trumpeter on the relief from the temple of Ramesses III carried his two instruments. At Kawa we are in no doubt about the identity of the objects: first of all, real incense-burners are carried by the priest preceding the group; second, the word 'trumpet' is written above the musicians. It is perhaps significant that the trumpeters remain silent, while the drummers and the harpists play. One of the latter appears to be beating the body of the instrument with a piece of wood, but perhaps he is playing with a large plectrum. The drums here are called *srh*. The singer walking between them while 'singing to the harp' is possibly blind, for he holds on to the waist of one of the drummers. This scene from a remote Nubian temple, along with a similar one decorated by the same king at Sanam, are the last examples of Egyptian military music in its proper context.

It should be mentioned that military music continued on Egyptian soil after the last of the Egyptian pharaohs, particularly during the Graeco-Roman period. A text found in Egypt mentions a military 'kornix', and the Etruscan and Roman versions of a trumpet known as 'lituus', 'cornu' and 'tuba' were also employed in Egypt. So was the Roman 'bucina', a horn used in the Roman army. With the exception of the forty 'horns' sent to Akhenaten (see above), there is otherwise little evidence of the use of horns as musical instruments in Egypt. The suitability of drums and trumpets and horns for military and processional functions, first realised by the Egyptians, was also exploited by other civilisations and continues to the present day: no military band would be complete without a brass section or drums to emphasise precision and supremacy.

6
Music at the court of Akhenaten and Nefertiti

The seventeen years of the reign of King Akhenaten (1367–1350 BC) were undoubtedly the most remarkable in the course of Pharaonic history. The king was the instigator of religious and social reforms which left a significant impression on contemporary art and literature, but had little influence on his successors. He propounded ideas which had been subtly foreshadowed during the reigns of his father and grandfather, placing increasing importance on the role of the Aten (sun-disc) in the religious affairs of his day. Akhenaten carried this emphasis to extremes, declaring the Aten sole god of Egypt and installing himself as the god's high priest. He undertook to subjugate most of the remaining gods of the Egyptian pantheon, above all Amun, who had been supreme royal god for centuries. Thebes and Memphis, the two main political centres, were obviously found to be too heavily burdened with relics of the past, and in about the fourth year of his reign Akhenaten began to transfer the court and administration to a locality now known as el-Amarna, half-way between the two cities.

The vast plain surrounded by desert mountains on either side of the river had not been used for a main settlement before, and this virgin soil was ideally suited for the location of the new capital, which was named Akhetaten (Horizon of the Aten). The city grew up with surprising speed, and included more than one large temple to the Aten, administrative buildings, residential quarters, palaces and, in the surrounding mountains, tombs for the high officials. A large tomb for the royal family was built in a remote desert valley. A few years into the reign of Tutankhamun, the boy king, the site was abandoned and attention was once more focused on Memphis and Thebes. The interlude at el-Amarna was deliberately obliterated from the record.

In modern literature the term 'Amarna Period' usually refers not only to the sojourn of the court at el-Amarna itself, but also to the early years of the reign before the move. Pictorial remains from buildings begun during these few years are numerous, and the evidence of musical activities is plentiful. The art of Tutankhamun's reign is also considered among 'Amarna' art, even though it may have been executed after the young king had left the city. Hence the Amarna Period spanned a mere twenty-five years, but in the visual arts it signifies nothing less than a revolution and in written sources the sun-disc gained a prominence which had long been suggested.

Representations of musical activities at this period can be found on the walls of officials' tombs, as well as on reliefs from the walls of the chapels of the Aten built by Akhenaten at el-Amarna and Karnak and Luxor too. The structures at el-Amarna were built of a soft, fine-grained limestone, which was easily carved into finely detailed reliefs; in contrast, the sandstone used in the Karnak region was of a much coarser grain, and the reliefs carved in it are consequently less crisp. In both cases the carvings were coated with a layer of gesso which received the detailed painted decoration. The blocks from el-Amarna, extracted from the foundations and core of later buildings in the 1930s, are now largely deprived of colour, but the quality of the reliefs is excellent. Stone from monuments at Karnak and Luxor, also reused in other buildings, are, however, in a less perfect state, but the numerous blocks taken from the ninth pylon of the temple of Amun at Karnak in the 1970s include many which retain their gesso and colouring.

There can be no doubt that music played a vital part in the life of the court of Akhenaten and Nefertiti, both at el-Amarna and during the crucial early years before the foundation of the new capital. There is some evidence to suggest that the princesses at the court of el-Amarna were familiar with musical entertainment: one representation of a harp-playing lady shows the elaborate wig and jewellery generally taken to denote royal status, although she remains nameless.

Representations of the palace at el-Amarna include views of the private quarters, so we are in the fortunate position of being able to look behind the scenes to witness music-making among the women of the harem. This was a separate apartment, guarded by door-keepers. Two halls with columns supporting the roofs provided the living quarters for the inhabitants during the day, with adjoining chambers for storing food and a large selection of musical instruments for entertainment. We know from the texts that a great many foreign ladies entered the harem of the king at this period, even when the king was himself a boy; some were sent by the King of Mitanni beyond the Euphrates. The foreigners seem to have lodged apart from the native women, but both groups are seen to be enjoying themselves, playing music, dancing, eating and arranging their hair. The Egyptians play the boat-shaped harp, lute, lyre and perhaps the double oboe; the foreigners substitute their native angular harp for the boat-shaped version, and in addition to lute and lyre a giant lyre can be seen in one of the adjoining chambers.

It is possible that some of the female musicians depicted in the harem were of royal blood, although in these private surroundings they have no distinguishing marks. An instrument appropriate for a lady of noble birth was the sistrum, the cult rattle of

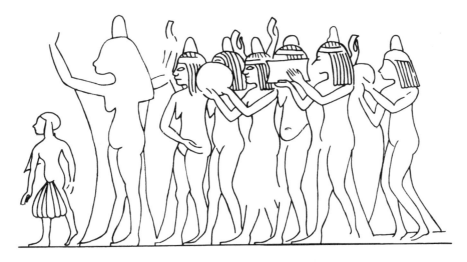

49 Street musicians. Tomb of Tutu at el-Amarna.

85

50 The harem of Akhenaten. The girls play angular and boat- shaped harps, lute and lyre.

priestesses and princesses. It had previously had strong connections with the goddess Hathor, and the rattle was adorned with her effigy. This was not allowed at el-Amarna, and the instrument was deprived of this characteristic element. Instead the handle was shaped like a papyrus stem. The function of the sistrum remained unaltered: to be shaken in front of a deity, in the present case the Aten. Queen Nefertiti herself is described in the tomb of one of the officials of the reign as the one who 'unites her beauties and propitiates the Aten with her pleasant voice and with her beautiful hands holding the sistra'.[23] The sistrum was essentially a feminine instrument, although in the Middle Kingdom it was a male priest who was in charge of instructing the priestesses in the art of sistrum-shaking.

Two sistra included in the burial of Tutankhamun present some puzzles. They differ from the many other surviving sistra in that, in accordance with the concepts of the period, they are stripped of any extraneous decoration. They are also made of gilded wood and bronze, instead of being entirely of bronze or faience, and they are unusually long at about 52cm. More interesting than their size is the fact that they are virtually identical and are probably to be considered a pair. Why would these two sistra have been included in the burial of the king? Even though the handles are made of wood, there is no reason to suppose that they were made only for funerary purposes: marks on the instruments suggest that they had actually been used. The funerary equipment of Tutankhamun remains enigmatic, especially since no comparable find has been made, so we do not really know what a full royal burial would have contained in normal circumstances. One rather has the feeling that any left-over items from the Amarna Period, whether funerary or not, were buried with the young king, because his death symbolised the end of an era. Perhaps these instruments belonged to a female member of the family, one of the ladies we see on the monuments shaking her sistra under the rays of the sun.

This was certainly the case with other instruments from the same tomb – a pair of tiny arm-shaped clappers inscribed with the names of the mother and eldest daughter of Akhenaten (see Plate 15). Unlike sistra, clappers are never shown being played by royal ladies. In the Amarna Period they were used by men in processions to spur on dancers and other performers. The men bend their backs at right angles, holding one clapper in either hand. Their instruments, which are undecorated, appear to be made in the shape of an ivory tusk. The royal clappers have the same profile, but terminate in a human hand and so may have a different purpose, being cult objects rather than true musical instruments: the rays of the sun were also shaped like a human arm in representations of this period. In fact, neither the sun's rays nor the sun itself as a cosmic element had been depicted before. In the 5th Dynasty (2494–2345 BC), which in many respects provided the inspiration for the sun cult of the Amarna Period, hand-shaped cult objects had a second role as musical instruments, seen for example in the mirror dance performed in honour of Hathor. The hand-shaped object was held up to be reflected in a mirror which, incidentally, was identical in shape to the sun-disc. It is possible that the clappers from the tomb of Tutankhamun served this double purpose. Another pair of hand-shaped clappers, found among the ruins of the palace at el-Amarna, appear to have been accorded reverential treatment: they were carefully wrapped in linen and placed in a box, almost in the manner of a relic.

Through the ages music has been considered the ideal pastime for noble ladies, but at the same time it has had erotic connotations. A scene from el-Amarna evokes an ambience quite different from the ritualistic cult-like atmosphere of the palace. It is set on the banks of a river where a state barge, manned by several sailors, sails against a backdrop of papyrus thickets. In the foreground one of the royal ladies entertains us on her lute, though she appears to be positioned in front of the vessel rather than on board. Musical boating excursions must be as old as music itself: Meketre, chancellor of one of the kings of the 11th Dynasty, brought his harpist and

51 An Amarna princess with a sistrum. Building of Akhenaten at el-Amarna. The Brooklyn Museum, New York (60.197.6).

singer along in his boat, and later ages witnessed riverine journeys with distinctly erotic undertones. The context of this scene has vanished with the neighbouring blocks, but there is evidence to suggest that not all erotic symbolism had been swept aside in Akhenaten's attempt to reshape the world. In the Amarna Period the coded language formerly used to express the wish for rebirth in the hereafter was generally abolished, but our river scene is not the only example to suggest that it continued nevertheless. A fragment of a ring bezel found in the city of el-Amarna shows a lute-nist playing in the company of a vervet (a species of monkey), a common symbol of female sexuality and part of the imagery of rebirth. Perhaps this piece was a family heirloom from the previous reign: there is, after all, a world of difference between a tiny personal object and an official monument, like the one on which the riverine scene appears, and it is at present difficult to assess the significance of the lute-playing princess in the scheme of decoration. It is possible that the relief came from the palace rather than from the temple.

It is interesting that musical representations on the monuments of the Amarna Period relate largely to the royal sphere. In private tombs such scenes rarely reflect the life and milieu of the tomb owner, and even in the Aten temples the decoration seldom shows music being played directly before the god. In tomb and temple alike representations centre on the royal family, and the king in particular. The musical ensembles are depicted within larger representations of the royal palace. These ensembles are closely related to those which we are accustomed to seeing in the ban-queting scenes of earlier periods (see chapter 2).

Among the musicians represented in the palace ensembles three main groups can be recognised: female Egyptians; male Egyptians; and male foreigners (probably Syro-Palestinians). As we have observed, foreign women can be seen playing instru-ments in some representations, but they are not shown performing in public, unless they are disguised in Egyptian wigs and costume. However, the evidence may be am-biguous here. The garments worn by foreign females vary from simple long kilts and Egyptian-style long tunics to the triple-tiered skirts worn by Asiatic men, and it is possible that in some fragmentary scenes, where the heads are missing, musicians interpreted as male could actually be female. This could be the case particularly in one instance where a group of foreigners playing lutes and a lyre is immediately fol-lowed by a girl playing a boat-shaped harp and wearing an Egyptian tunic.

The ensembles of Egyptian girls resemble female groups of the earlier part of the 18th Dynasty, except for variations in hairstyle. Since their garments were painted on the layer of gesso which has now largely vanished, they appear to be naked – the sensual character of Amarna art is here accentuated by the decay of the painted sur-face. The instruments played in these scenes have been taken from conventional ban-quet music: the boat-shaped harp, lute, lyre and double oboe. But in the Amarna Period the strings are given more emphasis, so that occasionally the harp and lute are doubled, and the wind instrument may be omitted altogether, although on the coarse sandstone reliefs the thin vertical lines delineating the instrument may easily escape notice. One girl in the group may also be clapping her hands. Some innovations in the forms of the instruments have taken place; for example, on the lyre the knob at the end of the yoke may imitate a cornflower or poppy seed capsule. More signifi-cantly, there may be changes in the construction of an instrument: it is at this time that a waisted lute is first seen, anticipating the shape of a modern guitar. The angular harp, which had appeared just once in a wall-painting from the reign of Amenophis II, is shown on a few occasions at el-Amarna. A new technique of blowing the double oboe is apparent at this time: instead of holding the two tubes at an angle and covering the holes of the tubes with the fingers of either hand, the musician now grasps the two tubes with one hand at the upper end, where there are no holes, leaving the other hand to cope with the hole (or holes) at the lower end of both tubes. This method of playing survived into the Ramesside Period, and it must have meant that a different range of notes could be obtained as well as a different combination of notes from either tube.

The Egyptian male musicians shown performing in the palace are found only in reliefs from Karnak; they are not known at el-Amarna, either in the tombs or from the Aten temples. They are distinguished by a white band that they wear over their eyes. This is a practice peculiar to the Amarna Period, and it applied to foreign male musicians as well. The significance of the blindfold will be discussed further in chapter 7, but its use among male musicians makes it possible to identify fragments of scenes and those showing men without instruments as belonging to a musical context. The heads of the men are closely shaven and they wear short or calf-length kilts.

Male Egyptian musicians are shown in two types of ensemble. In one their instruments include the large boat-shaped harp, otherwise played mainly by women, the lute and the lyre. Only the absence of the double oboe distinguishes these male ensembles from the female groups. It is possible that there were other distinctions which we can no longer recognise, such as tuning, but at this period there was a strong tendency to eliminate the differences between the sexes: in art the male adapts to the female in the sense that men are depicted with forms and curves previously used to characterise women. This 'unisex' principal may have been applied to conventional banquet music too.

The other form of ensemble was reserved for men alone, and it must have been invented by Akhenaten, for it was a totally new concept. It consisted of a large group of men clapping their hands and, presumably, chanting or reciting a verse, accompanied by a barrel-shaped drum. One group may have as many as seventeen members: groups of four, six and five men clapping, and a drummer, led by another

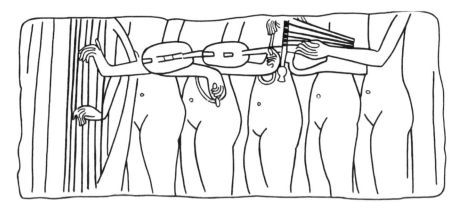

52 A female ensemble. Building of Akhenaten at el-Amarna. Norbert Schimmel Collection, New York.

53 Musicians. Temple to the Aten at Karnak: in the top register female musicians and male foreigners are depicted, in the bottom register, a large contingent of Egyptian clappers with the drummer, all of whom are blindfolded.

man clapping. It should be mentioned that these groups have so far been discovered only on blocks from the Aten chapels at Karnak. They are sometimes shown adjacent to foreign male musicians, but the proximity of the scenes does not necessarily mean simultaneous performance: the various ensembles at the palace are often separated only by a thin column, a separate register or by the simple device of turning the musicians to face in the opposite direction.

The barrel-shaped drum had hitherto been an instrument used by soldiers in procession in the open air. To transfer it to the inner regions of the palace was a novelty, and to combine it with the clapping of sixteen pairs of hands must have resulted in a performance of rare appeal. Sadly, we have no clue as to what they might have been chanting: the only hieroglyphs near the musicians give the word 'every'. Occasionally a lutenist mingles with such a group; in one scene a lutenist precedes two groups of four blindfolded men clapping, followed by ten more clapping men and a second lutenist. No drum is in evidence on this block, but the combination of lute and drum is known from the processional music in the late Amarna Period. In a fragmentary scene the group is shown below men whose arms seem to be lifted to carry an object, possibly a chair of a member of the royal family. Similar figures are shown on another block with a standing drummer and squatting men clapping.

The male foreign musicians wear a distinctive costume of pointed hat, a peculiar garment with long narrow sleeves, and a skirt bulging in three sections below the hips and reaching to the ankles or just below the knees. Foreigners introduced into Egypt an entirely new instrument: the giant lyre. The portable lyre, played by men and women in 18th Dynasty banquet music, was itself an import which continued to be used. The larger instrument, however, did not survive the reign of Akhenaten and it disappeared with the foreign musicians who brought it. It is interesting that the instruments shown on the temple reliefs from the Karnak area differ from those on the walls of the tombs at el-Amarna. Although the artists may have continued work on the temples of Karnak even after efforts were concentrated on the new buildings

54 Block from a temple to the Aten at Karnak showing, on the left, female musicians playing lyres, the oboe, the lute, and some are hand-clapping; on the right, in an adjoining room, foreign male musicians play the giant lyre and a portable lyre.

at el-Amarna, the scenes at Karnak are generally taken to antedate those in the new capital. The giant lyres at Karnak have a rectangular sound-box, like that of the portable lyre. The arms of the instrument are straight and symmetrical. The number of strings varies from five or six to fifteen, and they are fastened at the lower end to a square holder. The instrument appears to rest directly on the ground, reaching above the heads of the players, of which there are always two. The giant lyres shown at el-Amarna, however, have a different stringing arrangement. In the clearest representations there are eight strings, but the square string-holder is missing; instead, the strings terminate at a horizontal line below the upper edge of the sound-box, which is decorated with a design of calyx shape. Some of the lyres seem to retain their square sound-box, for the vertical lines of the arms are continued to ground level, but occasionally the square outline is missing, and it is tempting to read the calyx shape as a three-dimensional form rather than merely decoration. However, a lyre with a calyx- or vase-shaped sound-box is unlikely, and we should still visualise a fairly flat instrument, held upright and in balance by the two players. One of the Amarna lyres is provided with pegs at the yoke, a feature also evident on a few of the portable instruments.

The giant lyre offered new possibilities of an additional register of notes, which could be combined and alternated with those played on the smaller instrument. The concept of two players sharing one instrument was totally new in Egypt, and it poses once more the intriguing question of polyphony: were the strings of the giant lyre tuned symmetrically, so that each player plucked the same note at once, thus reinforcing the sound? Or were the strings tuned progressively, with the players plucking the strings in succession, or perhaps even simultaneously? Some of the instruments have an even number of strings, occasionally arranged neatly in two groups. But others show an uneven number, suggesting that unless two players shared the central string the tuning may not have been symmetrical at all. Furthermore, the hand of one player is shown reaching over to touch the strings in the other player's half, and we

91

55 Blocks from a temple to the Aten at Karnak showing various musical activities, including: a female ensemble; a male ensemble; foreign musicians playing a giant lyre. The performances take place beside offerings of food. In the top left corner, Queen Nefertiti presides.

shall probably have to imagine the ancient musicians as competent as modern pianists performing a duet.

Music clearly played a significant role in the cosmology of Akhenaten, since it was given such a prominent place in the decoration of the temples. Although the evidence from the walls of the Aten temples is fragmentary, enough research has now been carried out to ascertain that the musical ensembles depicted in the reliefs are playing in the palace. They are performing for the king, who was represented by his name if not present in person. But the king, who was the recipient of the music, was the embodiment of the Aten on earth, a mediator between the people and the deity. The scenes frequently include such accessories as items of food in jars or on stands, occasionally tended by servants who fan the jars to keep them cool, to ward off flies or perhaps to expedite the food's transmission to higher spheres. The god was believed to partake of the immaterial substances in the food offerings, while it was the priests and other personnel who actually consumed the meal, or passed it on to others. As in the 'Great Hymn to the Aten' (see below), a relation between food and music is spelled out over and over again, and it is as if music were chosen to symbolise the invisible (the immaterial substance/the sound) emanating from the tangible (the food/instrument). Life was a cycle of presentations: the god created the world and all that is in it for the king, who returned it to the god as an offering. The only other persons involved in this process, apart from a few servants, were the musicians who are positioned immediately in front of the offerings.

There are few scenes showing temple musicians playing directly to their god, compared to those of musical ensembles in the palace. They are depicted only in tombs, apparently where the decoration represents the entire temple of the Aten, and even then the general context is usually one of a royal visit to the temple. It is ironic that the temple reliefs do not actually contain any representations of temple musicians. Where they can be identified, they are invariably male, and are shown squatting in groups of three, four, eight or ten. One of them will play a stringed instrument, usually a medium-sized harp, although once a long-necked lute has been substituted. The harp is decorated with a royal head, as if the sound were understood to have emanated from the king's own body. It usually has a small number of strings (six or eight), although in one case it has as many as twenty. The musicians without instruments are shown clapping their hands and singing, but as it is often impossible in Egyptian art to distinguish between simultaneous and consecutive acts the clapping may have punctuated rather than accompanied the singing.

The temple musicians are shown playing to the Aten in an otherwise deserted temple, in an open courtyard directly under the sun. They appear to have performed only when the royal family had not yet entered the temple. Hymns to the Aten have survived, recorded on the walls of the officials' tombs. The author of the so-called 'Great Hymn to the Aten' took his inspiration from earlier hymns to other deities, hailing the god as creator of the world. In the hymn the king addresses the god directly, and it would seem a logical assumption that it was performed by the temple singers in the absence of the king himself:

Splendid you rise, O living Aten, eternal lord!
You are radiant, beautiful, mighty.
Your love is great, immense.
Your rays light up all faces.
Your bright hue gives life to hearts;
When you fill the Two Lands with your love.
August god who fashioned himself,
who made every land and created what is in it.
All peoples, herds and flocks,
All trees that grow from soil.
They live when you dawn from them,
You are mother and father of all that you made.

. . .

Singers, musicians, shout with joy,
in the court of the sanctuary
and in all temples in Akhetaten,
the place of truth in which you rejoice.
Foods are offered in their midst,
Your holy son performs your praises,
O Aten living in his risings,
And all your creatures leap before you.
Your august son exults in joy,
O Aten living daily content in the sky.[24]

56 Temple musicians. Tomb of Meryre, el-Amarna.

In one scene from the tomb of Meryre eight squatting musicians are joined by four men who stand facing the opposite direction and clap their hands. All the men in this scene are bald, and their kilts and tunics indicate that they are persons of some social standing. The sculptors have rendered the details of the faces with great sensitivity, from their bony skulls to the lines in their faces. Some of them have their mouths open as if singing; others press their lips together but their flaring nostrils suggest that they may be humming. All of the eight squatting performers are shown with clearly deformed eyes. This point is of particular interest. These blind temple musicians are found only on funerary monuments from el-Amarna, but they seem to bear some relationship with the blindfolded male palace musicians, whom we know only from Karnak. It must remain an open question as to whether the depictions reflect reality or whether artistic convention plays a role here. Unlike the representations from el-Amarna, the Karnak reliefs are not of sufficiently large scale to be able to show a deformed eye, and the only way to indicate abnormal eyesight would have been by a symbolic blindfold. The ambiguous nature of Egyptian art makes it difficult to find a definitive answer to this question. The significance of the blindfold is discussed further in chapter 6.

In the representations the musicians remain anonymous. There is usually nothing to indicate that any of them belonged to the royal family, although in one or two isolated cases they wear elaborate dress that would suggest noble or royal status. For information about the identity of some of the songstresses of the Aten we have to turn to personal items, such as the funerary figurines known as *shawabti*-figures. These were buried in great numbers in the tombs, and were believed to carry out manual labour on behalf of the deceased in the hereafter. The funerary beliefs of the citizens of el-Amarna remain obscure, but these figures continued to be made. They are conventionally inscribed with the name and title of the owner, and it is thanks to these little monuments that we know of the existence of Hatsheryt, songstress of the Aten, and her colleague Isis. Whether these ladies held office at el-Amarna itself is, however, not known, for the provenance of the figurines has not been established beyond doubt.

One musician who would have been at home in the temple of the Aten at el-Amarna can be seen in quite a different context. In the reign of Akhenaten or immediately afterwards a certain Paitenemhab prepared his tomb near Memphis in the north. The influence of the Aten was less significant away from el-Amarna, and it is really only perceptible in the expressive style of the relief and in the name of the owner, which includes the name of the sun-disc (Aten/Iten). The tomb chapel, which

57 Blind harpist. From the tomb of Paitenemheb at Saqqara; 18th Dynasty. Museum van Oudheden, Leiden.

is now in Leiden, is adorned with conventional funerary scenes. But the scene show-ing Paitenemhab and his family at the funerary banquet has a musical accompani-ment which bears little relation to light entertainment and shows much stronger links with the music of the Aten temple performed by grave, male musicians. The ensemble includes a harpist (Fig.57) and lutenist with deformed eyes, shaven skulls and pleated tunics, and two musicians playing the *nây*. The two flutes, not represent-ed at el-Amarna, hark back to ceremonial music of the years immediately before the revolution. The musicians, however, have normal eyesight and short hair, and wear kilts; there is nothing sacred about their appearance. The words of the harpist's song, preserved around the figures on the relief, contain no reference to the Aten. Its theme recalls earlier harpists' songs concerning the futility of life. The sphere of the king in his universe at el-Amarna has been left behind, but the image of the blind harpist, embodying musical performance in the temple of the Aten, stands out strongly on this monument erected hundreds of miles from the source of its inspiration.

1 (*above*) An erotic
music lesson? The
Brooklyn Museum,
New York (58.34).

2 (*right*) Drum
found at Thebes;
Late Period.
H. 37.1cm. Louvre
(N 1442), formerly
Salt Collection.

3 Old Kingdom harps and flute. Relief from the tomb of Kaemremet. Ny Carlsberg Glyptotek, Copenhagen (AIN 1271).

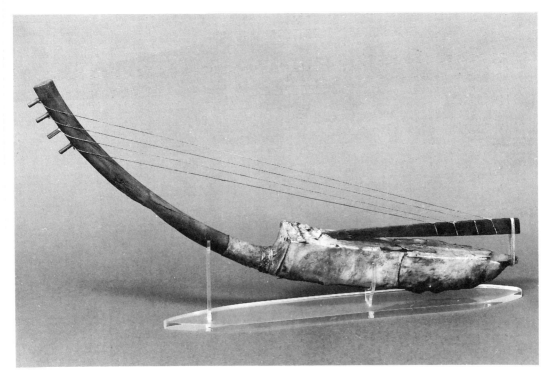

4 Portable boat-shaped harp; 18th Dynasty. British Museum (38170).

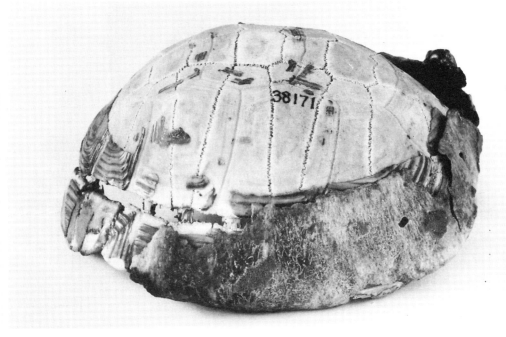

5 Tortoiseshell lute; New Kingdom. British Museum (38171).

8 The stela carried by the figure of Mahu; late 18th Dynasty. British Museum (22557).

9 Steatite bowl showing the festive procession along the exterior surface; 5th century BC?
British Museum (47992).

10 Cymbals; Roman Period. British Museum (6710).

11 Sistrum; Late Period. British Museum (36310).

12 Tambourine membrane; Late New Kingdom. Ashmolean Museum, Oxford (1890.543).

13 Crescent-shaped harp; Late Period? Oriental Institute, University of Chicago (27325).

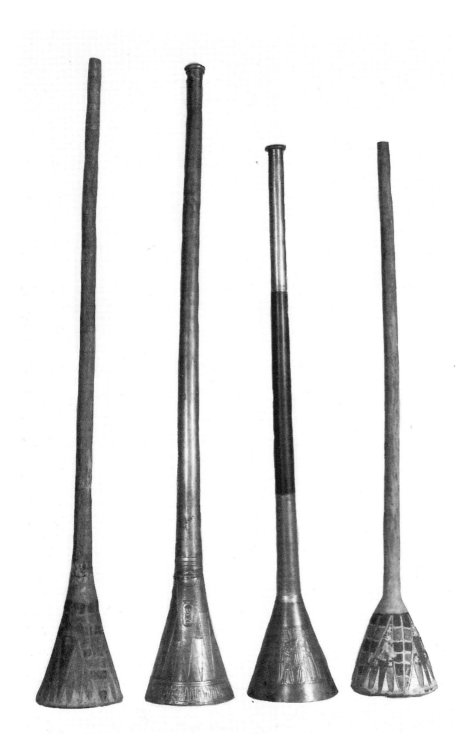

14 The trumpets of Tutankhamun with their wooden cores; end of the 18th Dynasty. Egyptian Museum, Cairo (CG 60850–1).

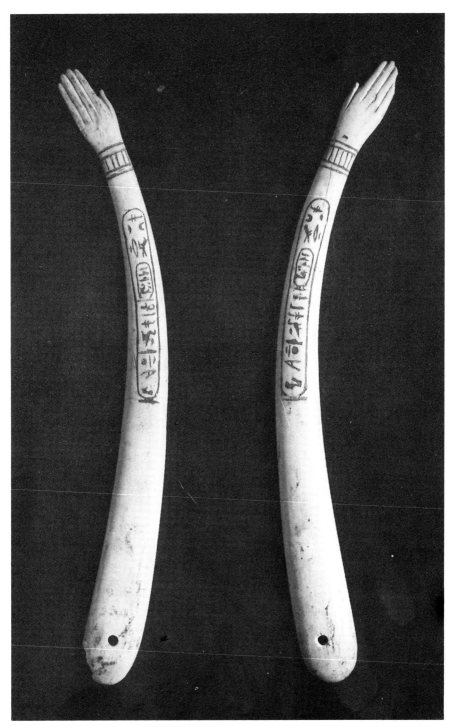

15 Clappers found in the tomb of Tutankhamun; end of the 18th Dynasty.
Egyptian Museum, Cairo (CG 69455a and b).

16 (*above*) Arched harp from
Thebes; New Kingdom. British
Museum (24564).

17 (*left*) Faience phallic figurine.
British Museum (M 39).

18 Wooden figurine of a girl with an angular harp; Ramessid Period. British Museum (48658).

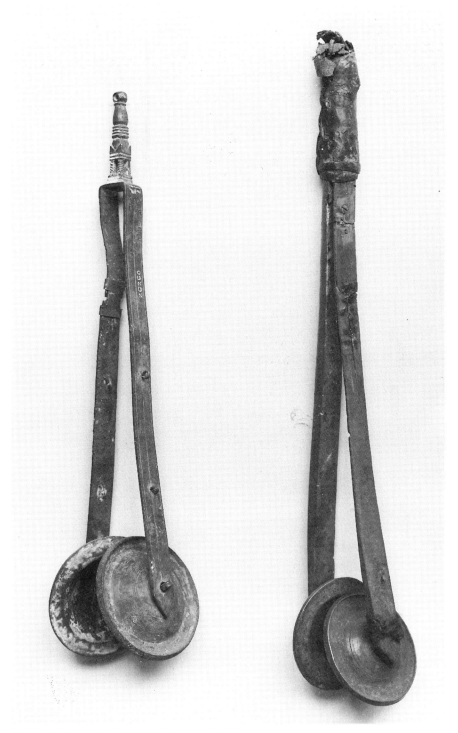

19 Crotals; Roman Period. British Museum (26260).

20 Statue of Pedekhons the lutist; Late Period. Fitzwilliam Museum, Cambridge (E.55–1937).

7
The blind harpist and his songs

I have heard these songs
which are in the ancient tombs,
which tell of the virtues of life on earth
and make little of life in the necropolis.
Why then do likewise to eternity?
It is a place of justice, without fear,
where uproar is taboo,
where no one attacks his fellow.
This place has no enemies;
all our relatives have lived in it from time immemorial,
with millions more to come.
It is not possible to linger in Egypt –
no one can escape from going west.
One's acts on earth are like a dream.
'Welcome safe and sound!'
to who ever arrives in the West.[25]

The 'Harper's Song' is an established genre in Egyptian literature in its various forms. One of its two main themes concerns reflections on life on earth as opposed to life in the hereafter. The songs to which the author of the above refers describe the futility of life, and the vain efforts made by the forefathers to secure eternity: their pyramids have collapsed, their houses have disintegrated. These songs invite us to spend a happy day, don our best garments, perfume our bodies, and enjoy music and dance with our nearest and dearest at our side. 'Chase away depressing thoughts, cheer up, and enjoy your brief life until death arrives' is the general message. The author of our song above has a few critical words to say to this. The hereafter is not an altogether undesirable place, and everybody is made welcome. In any case, it is no good fighting the inevitable: we shall all go to the place from which no one has returned. A second group of songs takes up this theme in detail and describes the situation of the tomb owner in his well-equipped tomb; his justification with the gods; and his eventual eternal existence in their company.

These songs are written in tombs of the New Kingdom from the end of the 18th Dynasty, but one is recorded on a papyrus scroll with the interesting addition that it is 'a song which is written before the singing harpist in the house of King Antef'. Kings of this name are known from the 11th, 13th and 17th Dynasties, but the wall-decoration in those of their tombs that have been identified includes no harpists. That the subject was not entirely unsuitable is proven by the fact that a later king – Ramesses III – chose to have not just one but two harpists depicted in a room of his

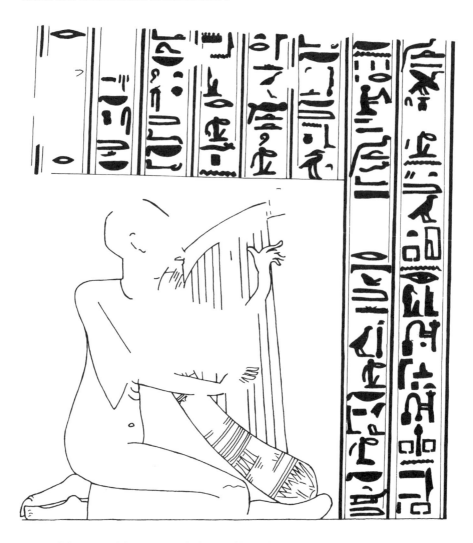

58 A male harpist with his song inscribed around him. Theban Tomb no.178 of Neferronpet; 19th Dynasty.

tomb (see below). The attribution to a specific 'King Antef' may be a literary technique, suggesting that the author needed to create a certain aura around his poem, and what could be better than an antiquarian touch?

As the song is copied on to a scroll among a collection of love poems, it may not necessarily have been intended for funerary purposes alone. In fact, excerpts from the song were used in the decoration of a toilet casket of the late 18th Dynasty showing scantily dressed female musicians before the happy owner of the container. It is interesting that the song is also found on the walls of Ramesside tombs, for this is exactly the period when we lose the banquet scenes which played such a prominent part in earlier tombs, as far back as the Old Kingdom. The music of the larger ensembles is now replaced by the song and its performer, conforming to a general trend which avoided scenes of 'daily life' and concentrated instead on religious topics. The

98

solo performer is most frequently a harpist, although occasionally he is replaced by a lutenist.

The important role of the solo harpist in Ramesside tomb decoration is antici- pated to some extent as early as the 18th Dynasty, when the scenes of banquet ensembles were at their peak. Already there was some indication that the player of the ladle-shaped harp (the instrument adopted by the solo harpist) might be dis- tinguished from other musicians. For example, he (or, more rarely, she) might be shown as a member of an ensemble, but is sometimes set slightly apart, perhaps in another register. Although he might be identical in appearance to the other male musicians, some representations make a distinction and show him with the characteristics which we now tend to attribute to The Harpist: the bulges on his sto- mach suggest that he was well nourished; his garments indicate an elevated status; and his bald head designates physical purity. He had become an established feature, and even in cases where the representation may be damaged and the instrument is gone, there is little doubt about his identity.

Another major characteristic distinguishes the harpist in some instances from his audience and fellow musicians: he is often shown with impaired vision, or even blind. Blind musicians are known from all civilisations, for to compensate for their handicap blind people develop extraordinary skills in other areas, and in literature the Egyptian harpist is often indiscriminately referred to as 'the blind harpist'. But the fact is that the number of representations which reveal impaired eyesight are rela- tively few, and other musicians, especially singers, may be shown in postures characteristic of blind people, possibly being led by others, or even with damaged eyes. The majority of the representations of known solo harpists come from the tombs at Thebes. Unfortunately, the inhabitants of the tombs during the past millen- nia have defaced many of the pictures of human figures on the walls, especially the eyes, so that most scenes cannot be investigated in this respect. However, out of some twenty cases where harpists' eyes were visible, only four or five were found to be ab- normal. In Egyptian art an 'abnormal' eye will be revealed by: (1) omission of the iris inside the outline of an otherwise normal eye; (2) representation of the eye as a nar- row slit with an iris; (3) depiction of the eye as a narrow slit without an iris; and (4) a line drawn following the upper curve of the eye. All of these may represent blindness, either with the eyeball intact and perhaps some sight remaining, or with a damaged or destroyed eyeball, where the muscles around the eye have contracted or sunk into the socket. Where the eye is shown as a narrow slit with an iris (2), the artist may simply have intended to show it half-closed; in those instances where the iris is omit- ted, it may originally have been painted in. Three representations of harpists in the Theban tombs show the narrow slit with iris, to which can be added a sketch on an ostracon; one has a narrow slit without the iris and the rest the single curved line: the conclusions which we can draw from this source are, therefore, ambiguous.

If we turn our attention to the monuments at el-Amarna, however, the situation changes dramatically. In art, as in other spheres, ideas current during the reign of King Akhenaten were highly exaggerated, and the extreme forms which they took can often suggest answers to problems which might otherwise remain enigmatic. There is no doubt that the musicians shown performing in the temple of the Aten at el-Amarna have deformed eyes with truly destroyed or shrunken eyeballs. These rep- resentations are most realistic and, together with the almost contemporary scene of

59 An artist's impression of
two blind musicians. Ostracon
from Deir el-Medina (2873);
Ramesside.

the harpist in the tomb of Paitenemhab at Memphis (see Fig.57), count among the masterpieces of Egyptian relief carving. The scenes were all depicted on the walls of private funerary monuments, and we should perhaps expect to find similar decoration on the walls of the temple itself, since this is obviously where these musicians were meant to perform. But strangely this is not the case, for neither the reliefs from the temples at el-Amarna itself nor those from the buildings at Karnak portray such blind temple musicians. The Karnak reliefs, however, reveal another interesting detail relating to this question: some of the musicians are shown wearing white blindfolds over their eyes. They perform in the palace itself, not the temple, for we also find entire scenes in the tombs of officials at el-Amarna which make the context clear. The male palace musicians all wear blindfolds while performing. As we have seen above, they play in groups which closely resemble the banquet ensembles of the earlier 18th Dynasty, but the context is now quite different: they appear to be taking part in offering rituals to the Aten and, since the setting is the palace and not the temple, to the king.

Judging from the evidence from Karnak and el-Amarna we must conclude that during such offering ceremonies male performers were not allowed to use their eyes. A blind man would be ideally suited to the part, and this was undoubtedly where such handicapped people found a true vocation. But the reliefs demonstrate that actual blindness was not required: temporary blindness, provided by the blindfold, was equally effective, perhaps even more so when depicted on the monuments, for in small-scale representation blindness would not show very well. Once their performance was over, the musicians would bow to the king, instruments in their hands, and push up their blindfolds. But what is the significance of the blindfold? While playing the musicians were in direct communication with the deity. Proximity to a divine being was believed in other early civilisations to cause blindness, but only to men; women had the privilege of being able to see the god. This was obviously the case with the Aten, for women are never blindfolded. The blindfold not only prevented the musicians from being able to see; they were also in a sense unseen, anonymous, almost non-existent while engaged in the ritual.

If we consider the implications of this, we shall have to question once more the actual blindness of the solo harpist. The evidence from Thebes indicated a certain proportion of harpists with apparently normal eyes. A recent discovery in the New Kingdom necropolis Saqqara, near Memphis, appears to support the idea that this alleged blindness could in some instances be symbolic, perhaps a way of expressing the might of a deity who had the power to blind ordinary mortals. Raia was chief singer of Ptah in the 19th Dynasty, and on the walls of his tomb he can be seen with perfectly normal eyes. But when he is depicted bending over his harp and singing to the god, something has happened to his visible eye, which has now become a narrow slit with a prominent supra-orbital ridge. Face to face with the god, Raia is blinded.

Thus we should not take it for granted that our solo harpist is actually blind in each and every case, whether he plays in the service of the god or for the entertainment of ordinary people. The Egyptian artist has managed to convey, however, that he was a very gifted musician, with his agile fingers moving over the strings and his back arching almost in imitation of the curve of his instrument.

As we have seen above, many of the characteristics of the solo harpist were becoming established during the early 18th Dynasty, but at this date he is neither blind nor anonymous: the singer Amenmosi, represented twice in the early tomb of Ineni, seems to have perfectly normal vision. Some of the typical attributes are even prefigured in the Middle Kingdom: one representation shows the portly figure and hunched posture of Neferhotep, who is portrayed on his stela, singing and plucking the strings of his harp (Fig.61). This is the fully developed image of The Harpist in the typical form in which he is depicted in the 19th Dynasty tombs, and it is perhaps one of the most striking examples. It remains an open question whether Neferhotep's eyesight was normal or not: the painted surface of the relief has faded, and the eye-socket is now blank.

The harp played by Neferhotep on his stela is an early form of the ladle-shaped type, which during the 18th Dynasty became the instrument of the solo harpist. During the Amarna Period it fell into disuse, perhaps because the musician who would have used it found himself out of work. The songs recorded in the 18th Dynasty are

60 Amenmosi the harpist. Wall-painting in Theban Tomb no.81 of Ineni, now largely destroyed. British Library (Hay MSS 29822,88).

61 Neferhotep, a blind harpist. Stela;
Middle Kingdom. Museum van
Oudheden, Leiden.

often dedicated to Amun, no doubt because the contexts in which they are found in
the tombs commemorate the Feast of the Valley, celebrated in honour of Amun.
When Akhenaten banned the cult of Amun, there was no further need for those who
sang the god's praise, and the instrument used on the occasion was presumably
remodelled to remove its unacceptable associations. The sound-box became shal-
lower, and any decoration at the tip of the neck now featured a king's head instead of
that of the goddess which had previously been preferred. The instrument in its new
form was used only in the most sacred of places: the temples of the Aten.

The harpist in the tomb of Paitenemhab plays an instrument which is rather similar to the Amarna temple singer's harp, except that it has the decoration of a bird's
head (a falcon?). With the beginning of the Ramesside Period the harp changes once
more, with two forms becoming apparent, one evidently derived from the ladle-
shaped harp, the other with the characteristic flat lower end of the 18th Dynasty
boat-shaped harp. There are many variations on these two basic types, and it is perhaps preferable to refer to them collectively simply as 'arched harps'. The neck of the
instrument is usually strongly curved, and the number of strings varies from six to
twenty-one. Like its ancestor, the harp may rest on a stand, and it is thus intended to
be played in a stationary position. It is a peculiar fact that just a single instrument has
survived, and this is rather an unusual specimen (see Plate 16). Now in the British
Museum, it is said to have come from the New Kingdom tomb at Thebes of a certain
Ani. The instrument is just under 100cm in overall length. As it appears to be of solid
wood, with no membrane covering the sound-box, it is considered to be a model.
The body is coated with a layer of painted plaster with some inlays in bone and
faience. The lower extremity has the decoration of a sculpted royal head, while the
tip of the neck has a hawk's head. The suspension rod has six holes, whereas the neck
originally had five pegs. The ratio between the longest and shortest strings suggests
an interval of no more than a fourth to be shared by the four strings.

The royal head on the sound-box is unusual, but it finds an echo in two of the most striking representations of musicians from ancient Egypt: the harpists in the tomb of King Ramesses III (Fig.62). When this tomb was first discovered in 1768 it became known as 'the tomb of the harpers'. It remains the only royal tomb with such a feature, but then Ramesses' tomb had other peculiarities too: several small rooms had decoration showing earthly activities, otherwise found only in tombs of ordinary people. As the tomb has been known and accessible from such an early date, its fragile wall-decoration has suffered greatly, and today only the upper half of the scenes remain. They were, however, copied early in the nineteenth century by, among others, the expedition of Robert Hay. The drawings, done by *camera lucida* or on tracing paper, must be considered the most accurate records of these remarkable paintings. They were positioned on opposing walls of a tiny room branching off from the central corridor of the tomb. The two harps are basically similar, but with different ornamentation, one having a royal head with the crown of Lower Egypt, the other, like the harp in the British Museum, showing a head with both striped head-cloth and double crown. The relation of the heads to the rest of the harp, and to the strings in particular, is not entirely clear, for the decoration depicted in the representations would have interfered with the strings. The harps are taller than their players and consist of a curved lower element, a straight intermediary piece and a strongly curved neck. The intermediary piece, as well as the lower part, must represent the total length of the sound-box, and both would have been covered with a membrane if the strings were to resound. There are eleven strings on one harp, thirteen on the other. The number of pegs in the Hay drawings is slightly confusing (ten and twenty-one), but fortunately the original painting still shows ten and eighteen pegs respectively. Assuming that the ancient artist had observed his subject correctly, these harps would have been capable of producing a fair range of notes, the ratio between the longest and shortest string being around 1:3 to 1:4 (i.e., 1 to 2 octaves). The gestures of the harpists are most expressive, one plucking strings 2 and 3, the other striking strings 1 and 4. The musicians are named as 'the harpist of the Underworld' and 'the harpist of Maat, mistress of the gods'. The face of one had been partially destroyed by the nineteenth century, but one eye of the other is clearly visible and is what we have described as 'abnormal', that is to say a narrow slit without an iris. Although the inscriptions refer to the song they sing, the actual words are left to our imagination.

The giant harps in the tomb of Ramesses III have a smaller counterpart in a drawing on an ostracon now in Cairo. The draughtsmanship is less expert, but this is an artist's freehand sketch on an uneven surface. The harpist, who has a deformed eye, plays a richly ornamented instrument provided with excessively large pegs. The purpose of such a drawing could have been to provide a preliminary sketch for the decoration of a tomb, or, alternatively, it could have been a copy done by the artist who had visited the tomb of Ramesses III, or had perhaps even been involved in its decoration. A second sketch of a blind harpist, now in the Metropolitan Museum of Art in New York, depicts a squatting musician such as those we have met in the private tombs. These examples certainly suggest that the subject of the blind harpist had a popular appeal. On official monuments, such as the walls of a tomb chapel, the draughtsman would generally have had little incentive to depict physical handicap, for his task was to present a perfect picture. In these sketches, however, he would have been free to depict his own personal view of the subject, and to him a harpist was blind.

62 The Harpist of Maat. Tomb of Ramesses III, Valley of the Kings; Late Period. British Library
(Hay MSS 29820,132; the draughtsman omitted to complete the feather pattern on the soundbox).

The songs of the harpists became a means of expressing in a poetical form some
reflections on important matters such as life and death. It may seem to us that the
ancient Egyptians placed more importance on the latter, for it is thanks to their careful preparations for life in the hereafter that we are so well informed of their life on
earth. Yet although one group of songs emphasises this view, the other encourages
its audience to enjoy life while it lasts. These thoughts were fitted into an existing lyr-
ical form: in hymns to the gods the Egyptians had been accustomed to addressing the
deity, describing him and giving him attributes which enabled them to explain and

organise the world around them. These ideas were delivered to the god in recitation, the attributes and qualities being given life through the spoken word. To serve its purpose the hymn had to be concise and rhythmical. The same applied to harpists' songs, and by analysing them we may be able to obtain some idea of the musical form in which they were presented. Instrumental music would either have accompanied the recitation or punctuated the various sections of the songs. In the course of time a specific musical form would have been created, which would have been paralleled in the words. If we can recognise a pattern in such texts, it would perhaps enable us to define the musical genre. The harpist's song in the tomb of Paser, vizier in the reign of Ramesses II, lends itself admirably to this exercise.[26]

INTRODUCTION
  [How weary is the nobleman.
  Good fate has become true.
  Verily, bodies have perished] since the days of the god,
  others taken their place.
  Those who built houses or pyramids
  rest in their necropolis

     . . .

A
  You excellent spirits who follow Osiris
  turn your faces to the mayor.
  See, he has come in peace
  Give . . .
  . . . truth
  which he brought to you so often
  as it rested on his chest and never left.

R Spend a happy day, Paser

     . . .

     . . .
  Follow your heart for as long as it is yours.

R Spend a happy day, nobleman.
  Ignore all evil and remember happiness
  until the day arrives when you moor
  in the land that loves silence.

  R Spend a happy day. Do whatever you praise.
    Let your heart be very, very happy.
    Anoint yourself with unguent for the divine body at
    Heliopolis.
    See . . .

B R Spend a happy day, nobleman.
    See, your fortune weighs heavier than posterity.
    If you are headed for
    your name will reach eternity through it.

  R Spend a happy day, O . . .

105

MAIN PASSAGE │ What god loves he will give to you.
│ Bread, beer, wine and unguent
│ will together
                                       . . .

   A │ Do not think of the day of 'come'
│ until you set out for the west like a praised one.
│ Look, what the priests scatter on the ground
└ what they place on the altars – what is it all for?

   R   Spend a happy day in the right way,
       multiply good.
       Look, fate does not increase its days.
       Time will come in due course, with nothing added.
       No one who went ever came back.

                       . . .

                       . . .

                       . . .

A close examination of the words reveals a repeated phrase, 'Spend a happy day', followed by two accompanying lines, the wording of which varies in each case. This
refrain occurs six times. A long introductory section is concluded by two such
refrains. Then there is a central section consisting of three refrains, which is followed
by a second longer section, counterbalancing the first, with a final repeat of the
refrain. Although the words of the second long section are different from those in the
first, the two sections form a symmetrical composition around the central section.
Hickmann, who studied this song with a view to tracing its musical form, was
tempted to label the long sections A and the central section B, giving a structure
A B A – which the musically trained person will have no hesitation in recognising as
the ternary form. We have already seen (chapter 1) that there is some evidence to suggest that a form akin to the rondo may have been in use in the songs of farmers from

63 Ensemble. Tomb at Memphis(?); Ptolemaic. Graeco-Roman Museum, Alexandria.

an early date. If we can recognise the set pattern in the cycle of theme and variations that the words of this song present, then a leap of the imagination can suggest the instrumental part that may have accompanied it.

The image of the harpist playing his instrument alone, portrayed in affluent maturity but not necessarily with noticeably impaired vision, survived the tradition of tomb decoration as we have met it, especially in the monuments at Thebes. He is depicted on a number of private commemorative slabs of wood in the Late Period (see chapter 8), and even in the Ptolemaic reliefs from Memphis (see above) the harpist in the group is not just any anonymous musician: his physical type is closely related to that of his ancestors of nearly two thousand years earlier.

8
Music and sexuality

Another aspect of the role of music in ancient Egypt is revealed in a quotation from a scribal school text of 19th Dynasty date (*c.* 1200 BC). Such texts were copies made by young Egyptians training to be scribes, and served to sharpen their skills in the complicated art of writing and, with luck, to familiarise them with the moral tenets that they contained. Frequently they glorified the scribe's career above all others, and castigated as abominations the idle lives of those who revelled in their senses. Among other things the student is advised never to touch wine, for it leads to drunkenness and the company of women of dubious reputation, who would even teach him to sing to the oboe and chant to the lyre. In the first century AD, over a thousand years later, music was truly forbidden fruit, if we are to believe Diodorus in what he wrote about the Egyptians: 'In ... music it is not customary to receive any instruction at all ... they consider music to be not only useless but even harmful, since it makes the spirits of the listeners effeminate'.[27]

Music and love go hand in hand in most civilisations, ancient as well as modern, and in different spheres – from the brothel to the temple. The two instruments singled out by the ancient schoolmaster in the scribal school texts occur elsewhere in

64 Erotic scene with a discarded lyre. Drawing on papyrus; Late New Kingdom. Egyptian Museum, Turin (55001).

65 Girl playing the oboe. Wall-painting in a house at Deir el-Medina; Ramesside.

quite respectable circumstances, but they are also among those known to have had erotic associations. A lyre, for example, was one of the accessories of the inhabitants of a 'house of pleasure' in the late New Kingdom, probably located at Deir el-Medina near Thebes in Upper Egypt. A papyrus scroll, now in the Egyptian Museum in Turin, makes the connection between music and the erotic even more explicit. On it are depicted a number of sexual episodes, and since they all feature various stages of intercourse among several different partners there can be little doubt about the general milieu. One of the women is just letting go of her musical instrument, which she must have used to entertain her client: it is a lyre decorated on the arms with horses' heads, and on the yoke with geese's or ducks' heads; the duck, as we shall see, was a well-known erotic symbol. Instruments of the same type have survived, although rather larger than the one depicted; two particularly beautiful examples are in West Berlin.

Another of the women on the scroll seems to have made use of a sistrum, which she has placed under her stool. The sistrum was usually a sacred emblem, carried by priestesses and noble ladies, and one is slightly surprised to come across it in such surroundings, though there is another case of a drunken lady waving a sistrum and emptying a jar of wine at the same time. In the adjoining scene on the Turin scroll a man has taken hold of the sistrum, carrying it with his arm stuck through the arch while his partner perches on a chariot. In his hand he holds a curious object, which is also depicted under the chair next to the sistrum in the previous scene. It seems to be

66 Lutenist. Drawing on a
piece of wood found in Theban
Tomb no.38; 18th Dynasty.

a vessel: could it be a container for fragrant oil, or would it perhaps have been used as a rattle with pebbles or dried beans inside? A sistrum may be paired with a *menat*-necklace, or an arched sistrum with a naos-shaped sistrum, but this combination is a novelty, intended, no doubt, to satisfy the senses in some way.

The provenance of the Turin scroll is not known for certain, but it probably came from Deir el-Medina, the village inhabited by the craftsmen who built and decorated the splendid royal tombs in the Valley of the Kings. A wealth of material has been discovered at Deir el-Medina which provides unique information about the lives of the people who lived there, including details of their seemingly promiscuous behaviour. (As similar material is not available from other sites it is not possible to judge how far their moral principles conformed to accepted standards.) Further illustrations on the relationship between sex and music can be found here. For example, a wall-painting dating from the late New Kingdom shows a woman dancing to her own accompaniment on the double oboe, which, as we have seen from the scribal school texts, had an ambiguous reputation. The oboist appears to be naked, though partly enveloped in leafy garlands and what appears to be a red shawl cast over her shoulder. On her thighs she has tattoos of Bes, the musical dwarf god who was the protector of women on the intimate occasions of conception and delivery. The painting was found in a private house, positioned near a plinth which may well have served the purpose of a bed, so it is tempting to interpret the room as one where either conception or delivery took place. The leafy garland is characteristic of scenes of childbirth, but it can also be seen in connection with intercourse, for example in the chariot scene in the Turin erotic papyrus.

Deir el-Medina has also yielded thousands of ostraca, flakes of limestone or sometimes pottery, an ideal and cheap medium for an artist's sketch. Produced by such skilled craftsmen, the drawings on these ostraca are often of high quality. A girl with a musical instrument would have provided an attractive motif for the ancient draughtsman freed from the conventions demanded for representations in tombs and temples, and among the favourite subjects was the lutenist. Her instrument was particularly suited to suggesting an erotic atmosphere. Unlike the boat-shaped harp of the time, it was small enough to be shown being embraced by the player, and it did not interfere with the face as a wind instrument would have done. In some cases the lute is even being played, or at least held, while sexual intercourse takes place. In one instance a female lutenist seems to have been taken by surprise during her rehearsal. Or perhaps this is an early version of the familiar theme of 'the music lesson'. We shall never know what prompted the draughtsman to jot down this charming drawing.

   In reality the player would have used the lute to accompany herself in her songs. These were sometimes prosaic, calling out the ingredients for a successful evening: 'Pieces of meat! Branches of acacia! Singers sweetly anointed!' Or we can imagine the songstress reciting one of the love poems for which the Egyptians were truly famous. One such lady is actually known: she was Tashere, who was attached to the music room of a mayor's children. One of her songs was recorded on a papyrus scroll during the New Kingdom, but the scribe claims to have copied it from an even older version which he found in a scroll case. This had been written down by a certain Sobknakht, who had been present at Tashere's performance. The lute, as we have seen

67 Lutenist and song.
Ostracon from Deir el-Medina;
Ramesside Period. Egyptian
Museum, Cairo (2392).

111

(chapter 2), would have been capable of a fair range of notes, and we can imagine Tashere beginning her song with the following lines:

> When you go to the house of the sister
> and charge towards her grotto,
> the gate is made high.
> Its mistress cleans it
> and furnishes it with the palate's delight,
> exquisite wines, specially reserved.
> You confound her senses(?)
> but stop at night when she says to you,
> 'Hold me tight that we may lie like this
> when dawn comes.'[28]

The erotic connotations of the lute are also strongly suggested by the decoration of a duck's head, which it sometimes bore. The role of animal symbolism is another intriguing aspect of the relation between music and the erotic. Several instruments have been mentioned as having animal decoration: the duck, horse, falcon, lion, ram and possibly also the antelope. The duck carried a specific erotic symbolism, which fits well with the context of some of the scenes, whereas for others any sexual association would be pretty far-fetched. However, in certain drawings from Deir el-Medina animals have been substituted for women in musical ensembles, and they occur in musical scenes which have a distinctly erotic ambience. On the Turin papyrus scroll, for example, the portion adjoining the section which depicts sexual activities shows illustrations of animal fables – beasts behaving as human beings. The main register here depicts an animal ensemble, headed by a donkey harpist. The lion plays a lyre, the crocodile a lute, and the vervet an oboe. A lute-playing crocodile also appears on a curious relief, entertaining a female mouse while a naked girl balances on his back and plays an angular harp.

It is interesting that in such drawings certain instruments are most often allocated to the same animal: the crocodile has the lute (it would be anatomically difficult to show it holding any other instrument); the hyena is given the harp or, more frequently, the oboe; the lion plays the lyre, which might itself be decorated with a lion's head. The oboe might also be played by the goat and the vervet. Only once do we see a donkey with an instrument (a harp), and a small barrel-shaped drum is in one instance beaten by a goat.

It is possible that a particular animal was chosen to play a given instrument because it was thought to express the character of that instrument. The truth of this surmise often still eludes us, but ancient sources seem to confirm that the vervet could perform such a function, since the animal appears in a number of erotic situations. For example, it is one of a range of sexual symbols on a blue faience bowl, now in Leiden. The design, in black lines, shows a naked female lutenist squatting on a cushion, while a vervet touches her hip belt. The lotus flowers, the unguent cone on her head, her elaborate wig, the Bes tattoo on her thigh all have erotic significance, and the lute by its very presence in such a setting would seem to have too.

For the other animals we have little evidence of any sexual significance, but they may have conveyed other associations. The lion, for example, was above all a royal creature, so we should perhaps rank the sound of the lyre accordingly. The

68 An animal ensemble including a goat with a drum and a hyena with a double oboe. Ostracon from Deir el-Medina; Ramesside Period. Egyptian Museum, Cairo (2844).

crocodile played many parts in myth and ritual, though rarely sexual, and in music only in the two examples quoted above. It was a powerful animal, feared by everyone. The sound of the lute was most probably believed to express these qualities, but it is difficult to see an immediate connection with an enticing naked songstress playing the same instrument (except that both may play in a recumbent position). The goat does not appear to have played a major part in popular belief, but it is interesting that in Thebes, where all the musical goats come from, an aspect of Amun manifested itself as a goat. This was 'the glorious *ba*' (inadequately rendered as 'soul'), precisely that area of his personality which would contain his sexual power. That the goat plays the 'erotic' oboe can be no coincidence, and we must assume that the Egyptians considered the sound of the oboe as capturing aptly this fundamental aspect of life.

Two animals are depicted playing the harp: the hyena and the donkey. Little is known about the role of the hyena in Egyptian folklore, but it was generally feared because of its rapacious habits. The donkey, in official sources, was seen as an embodiment of evil forces. Any connection with the gentle sound of the harp seems remote: in three cities trumpet-playing was banned because the sound was too reminiscent of a donkey's lamenting cry, and it was considered to be in bad taste to make flutes from donkeys' bones!

If these scenes do not offer definitive proof of the erotic aspect of the harp, an instrument generally heard in temples or at banquets, other situations are more explicit. Mention has already been made of The Brooklyn Museum limestone figurine of an ithyphallic male and harp-playing female (see p.14 and Plate 1). Phallic figurines such as the Brooklyn piece became quite frequent towards the end of the Pharaonic Period and in Graeco-Roman times, and it is not uncommon for them to take the form of a man playing an angular harp which rests on his phallus (see Plate 17). A variant of this subject, with a woman perched on the tip of the phallus, must have been particularly popular, for several such figurines exist, all cast from the same mould (only one is complete, now in Munich). The relation between sexuality and music can hardly be more clearly spelled out, yet without more evidence from literature it is difficult to assess the exact nature of this relationship.

The significance of the harp (see Plate 18) may be difficult to define precisely, but its function is unambiguously sexual in a coloured drawing on leather in New York's Metropolitan Museum of Art. This intriguing object was discovered during excavations at the temple of Deir el-Bahari on the west bank of Thebes, and has been described as a 'hanging', although it could have been part of a scroll. Only a corner remains, showing parts of two registers. In the lower register is a unique scene: a woman plays a harp to a man who is dancing around with erect phallus, waving what appears to be a whip or flywhisk. The setting includes plants, and others are present, for we can see the tips of their feet. The occasion is not easy to explain; it could be anything from an orgy like that on the Turin scroll to a ritual dance connected with fertility. The leather fragment was found near the temple where numerous votive phalli had been deposited by visitors in ancient times. The shrine was dedicated to Hathor, who was mistress of the necropolis, as well as the goddess to whom lovers addressed their prayers.

If the message of this representation is in the area of fertility rather than simple eroticism, the dividing line between the two is at times minimal for an ignorant spectator thousands of years later. Further evidence may perhaps be forthcoming from

69 Harpist. Painting on leather found at Deir el-Bahari; 18th Dynasty. Metropolitan Museum of Art, New York.

70 Mereruka's wife playing the harp. Tomb of Mereruka, Saqqara; 6th Dynasty.

the tomb at Saqqara of a certain Mereruka, vizier of King Teti around 2340 BC. A relief in the tomb shows Mereruka and his wife seated on the conjugal bed, an unusually intimate scene for this kind of monument. Elsewhere we may see the bed and head-rest laid out, and the prospective occupants preparing themselves, being anointed or having their hair dressed. But it is only in the exceptional case of Akhenaten and Nefertiti that we meet known and named persons about to retire. Mereruka's wife entertains him by playing her harp, while he waves his flywhisk, which is not dissimilar to the object carried by the man on the leather fragment described above. It has been suggested that the representation symbolises the consummation of the marriage between Mereruka and his spouse. It is possible to carry the interpretation further and say that it may refer to the underlying sexual forces of the couple, which will enable them to be reborn in the hereafter. Such symbolism is now well established for the Middle Kingdom and later, especially for the New Kingdom, and it appears to be based on even earlier concepts, contemporary with the monument of Mereruka. As we have seen (chapter 5), music seems to have played a part in transmitting nourishment from food offerings to the gods, and the harp here may have had a similar role in activating the erotic elements in a fertility ritual. This would indeed be its function in funerary beliefs, and it would provide a satisfactory *raison d'être* for music at the funerary banquet. To consider it as mere entertainment would be to underestimate the Egyptians' profound spiritual consciousness.

A wall-painting in the Theban tomb of Nakhtamun seems to confirm the suggestion of such a connection between music, sexuality and funerary beliefs. The persons providing the music for his funerary offerings are not the dignified ladies we see in 18th Dynasty banquet scenes, nor is it the lone harpist who graces so many New Kingdom tombs (see Fig. 26). Nakhtamun, who lived during the 19th Dynasty, chose a lyre-playing girl with prominent Bes tattoos on her thighs and a woman with a large boat-shaped harp. The lyre is decorated with a duck's or goose's head, and the heads of what are possibly two antelopes. We should not take the rather dishevelled look of the musicians as significant, for many ladies in Ramesside paintings have the same appearance, but the Bes tattoos are indicative of their role. We may perhaps compare the scene with a wooden figurine of a girl playing a six-stringed angular harp. The fact that the tip of the instrument has been inserted into her vulva is hardly unintentional. The girl's breasts and shoulders appear to be covered in tattoos, unless the markings are meant to represent a necklace. The nipples and pubic triangle are emphasised and suggest that the girl is naked. The figurine must have served a funerary purpose, being deposited in the tomb of an Egyptian more than three thousand years ago.

A passage from Herodotus, dating from the fifth century BC, shows how the erotic associations of music may have been manifested on other ritual occasions. He describes an episode during the annual Feast of Bastet in her Delta residence of Bubastis. Bastet was a cat goddess, whose attributes overlapped to some extent with those of Hathor. She was associated by the Greeks with their Artemis (goddess of hunting), although significantly they also called her Aphrodite (Greek goddess of love). We might, therefore, expect celebrations in her honour to be uninhibited, as Herodotus indeed reports:

> When the people are on their way to Bubastis they go by river, men and women together, a great number of each in every boat. Some of the women make a noise with *krotala* [clappers], others play *auloi* [double oboe] all the way, while the rest of the women, and the men, sing and clap their hands. As they journey down to Bubastis, whenever they come near any other town, they bring their boat near the bank; then some of the women do as I have said, some shout mockery of the women of the town, others dance, and others stand up and expose their sex. This they do whenever they come beside any river-side town. But when they have reached Bubastis they make a festival with great sacrifices, and more wine is drunk at this feast than in the whole year besides.[29]

The shrill sound of the oboe was to become a well-known feature on Greek soil in a number of different circumstances, but notably in rather explicitly erotic contexts: it was able to arouse the phalli of a herm (a pillar with a head and genitals) and dancing *silenoi* (Bacchus' attendants); its erotic associations in Egypt have already been examined.

The crotals mentioned by Herodotus have been encountered in the discussion of religious music (chapter 4, and see Plate 19). Crotals were miniature cymbals attached to a pair of handles and thus combined the characteristics of clappers and cymbals. The latter were also used in the ritual sphere from at least the Middle Kingdom, but by the Hellenistic Period, according to the third-century AD Alexandrian writer Athenaeus, they were considered to be a symbol of depraved effeminate life. Their tinkling sound was said to accompany indecent gestures and shameless acts. In scenes dating from the New Kingdom one-handed clappers appear in the hands of women dancing in the street, and they are occasionally used by girls performing with banquet ensembles: it would seem that the festival spirit already expressed itself by the use of the instruments recognised by Herodotus some thousand years later.

Further evidence of the erotic character of certain musical instruments can be found in the official sphere of temple architecture. Although we must move forward in date to the Graeco-Roman Period, the nature of the evidence remains purely Egyptian, for the foreign rulers of Egypt adapted to Egyptian traditions in building monuments for Egyptian gods in Egyptian style, far removed in concept and appearance from the conventions of their own native civilisation. On the island of Philae south of modern Aswan, next to the grand temple of Isis, was a small temple to Hathor. At Thebes we see this complex goddess as lady of the necropolis, but at Philae it is the more benign aspect of her personality which is celebrated. According to one myth, Hathor resided in the desert as a ferocious lioness. Re, the ancient sun-god and Hathor's father, became embarrassed by her brutish lifestyle. He decided to bring her home to Egypt, but this was no easy task, and he required the skills of Thoth, god of magic. Hathor was lured home by a magic potion, backed up with promises of a life dedicated to music, song, dance and drunken happiness. The first port of call on the journey home was Philae, and it is this event which is celebrated in her temple on the island. She is received by priests playing harp and oboe, and priestesses with sistra and flowers. The savage lioness is transformed into the beautiful, gentle goddess of love. It is in this capacity that she presides over the birth-house (see chapter 4).

The forecourt of her temple at Philae contains two rows of columns, partly engaged in the walls, and here we find representations of music-making. The performers consist of women, monkeys and figures of Bes, one on each column, represented twice. The women play double oboe and lyre – we are again reminded of earlier references to precisely these two instruments as played by women. The oboe in these reliefs is held in a curious fashion, each hand clasping one of the tubes as if no finger-holes existed, except that one little finger sticks up in the air. This is a strange contrast with the way in which the New Kingdom artists depicted the musicians' agile fingers running up and down the tubes. The lyre is exceptionally large, so heavy in fact that a table has been provided for it to rest on, reminding us briefly of the giant lyres of Akhenaten, though these were of a different construction. The lyre of Hathor has a trapezoidal sound-box and arms shaped like papyrus columns. The fourteen strings are fastened to a rectangular string-holder at the base of the instrument. On one representation the upper part of the instrument is complete, and we can see the cushions or splinters of wood used for tuning; a cow's head decorates the yoke. The lyre-player plucks one string with each hand, unlike her New Kingdom colleague, who would have spread out one hand to deaden some of the strings while flicking her plectrum deftly across all the strings with the other. The sound quality of a lyre played without a plectrum rather resembles that of a harp.

The monkey holds his lute without actually playing it. It is of the elongated, wooden type. The neck of the instrument is not decorated with a duck's head, but with what appears to be the head of Hathor seen *en face*. This monkey is not the little vervet but a full-grown baboon, sacred animal of Thoth.

117

The angular harp played by Bes is a splendid instrument with nearly twenty strings, and the god manages to perform dancing steps while playing. He is also shown beating the round tambourine to Hathor, his mistress. The presence of Bes should not surprise us, for the sexual connotations of this context are entirely appropriate for him.

The instruments used in the celebrations of the goddess of love were thus lyre, angular harp, lute, double oboe and round tambourine. These must have been especially joyful instruments, for with the exception of the lute they are precisely the ones which were banned on the sites where Osiris, King of the Dead, was buried. According to mythology, Osiris was torn to pieces by his brother Seth and his body scattered; several shrines in various parts of Egypt therefore housed his remains. One of them was on the island of Biga, immediately opposite Philae. It was so sacred that any frivolous activities were forbidden there. A decree was set up, carved in stone, making this absolutely clear, and among other things we read: 'Do not play the tambourine here, nor sing to the harp and oboe.'[30]

At Abydos, further north, a similar restriction was reported by Strabo, the geographer, when he arrived there around the beginning of the Christian era, for he says: 'In Abydos they venerate Osiris, and in the temple of Osiris no singer nor oboe-player nor lyre-player is allowed to make music for the god, as it is the case for other gods'.

We have seen in chapter 4 that music did indeed play a part in the ritual performed to the gods. In Graeco-Roman Egypt other instruments existed apart from those mentioned in the decrees, and they were not specifically excluded. We may perhaps deduce that the angular harp, lyre, oboe and tambourine were so established in the cult of Hathor that they could not be played unless a sexual purpose was intended, be it procreation or rebirth. In the Middle Kingdom the (arched) harp had been an item of funerary equipment, included in the 'ideal list' depicted on the inside of wooden coffins, an instrument to be used in the transformations of the dead, and it reappeared in sexual contexts at various levels. The lute, which was omitted in the decree,

71 Performers playing the lyre, lute and tambourine. Temple of Hathor, Philae; Ptolemaic.

72 Playing the tambourine to Bes;
Ptolemaic. Relief seen on the art market
in 1984.

turns up in the wall-decoration of the birth-house (*mammisi*) at Edfu. The tambourine, first on the list in the decree, is shown extensively being played by goddesses in
ceremonies surrounding birth, as in several birth-houses, or, at a more popular level,
played directly before Bes by naked females.

In the light of this evidence, it is clear that many of the musical scenes with an
explicit or implicit sexual message formed an important element in ceremonies concerned with life, death and rebirth. The role of music in religious and funerary practice was considerable, and many of the sexual representations must have had a
deeply symbolic rather than purely erotic significance.

9
The musician in society

The preceding chapters have shown that Egyptian monuments abound with depictions of musicians singing and playing. Together with the evidence of surviving instruments, these representations can give many clues about the music played in ancient Egypt, even about the kinds of sounds which may have been produced, and they certainly tell us much about the occasions on which music was deemed essential. But what can we learn about the musicians themselves, and their place in society?

The names of Egyptian individuals which have come down to us through their own monuments represent a wide spectrum of society. We know viziers, treasurers, generals and mayors, but also workers and craftsmen, barbers and military recruits, and a great many priests and government officials. Such people had the means to commission stelae, statues or even decorated tombs in their own honour, and these records have often survived thousands of years until the present day. But when one studies the range of professions represented by the titles of the owners, it is difficult to avoid wondering how some of them came to achieve such glory. Wealth was certainly one criterion, but personal merit might entail a royal gift in the form of a funerary monument of some description. Public monuments in honour of private individuals were the exception and one would have had to achieve the status of a semigod to deserve it. This means that excellence in a particular field would be recorded for posterity only if it gained royal recognition, or if the person in question were sufficiently affluent to take the matter in hand himself.

Able musicians might achieve considerable status. Not only were they master performers, but they probably composed their music too. Skilful performances could win a high reputation, and some solo musicians were sufficiently rewarded financially to be able to afford important monuments of their own. Others are known from monuments of other people, often depicted with fellow members of an ensemble, notably on the walls of tombs. However, considering the large number of representations of musicians, very few can be identified. Some ensembles are shown with the players' names written next to them, and in these cases we must assume that they represent groups which actually existed. Where the participants remain anonymous, it is much more likely to be a conventional 'ideal' scene.

In the Old Kingdom the musicians depicted in the tombs are occasionally relatives of the owner, usually performing on a harp. The earliest date at which we can begin to put names to professional musicians is the mid-5th Dynasty. Nikaure was a judge and inspector of book-keepers, but he held some priestly titles as well. A corner of the false door in his tomb at Saqqara is dedicated to a representation of two people he must have known and appreciated in real life: the harpist Hekenu and her singer and chironomist, a woman called Iti. These two must have formed a famous duo, for it was a rare honour to be thus commemorated in someone else's tomb, especially on the false door, the focal point of the tomb. Iti is not to be confused with a male name-sake who had a tomb at Giza. This man was one of a number of persons holding the title 'overseer of singing in The Great House [the palacc]'. He was later succeeded in office by a certain Nimaetre, who was in charge of the musical entertainment at the palace. Perhaps the first such 'overseer' (ỉmy-r) known to us was Khufuankh, who had a tomb at Giza. He appears to have lived at the beginning of the 5th Dynasty, although the late 5th Dynasty has also been suggested. The main feature in his tomb was the false door, establishing its owner's identity in text and pictures. Among Khu-fuankh's titles were 'overseer of singers in The Great House' and 'overseer of flau-tists', but he is not actually shown performing. The text specifically states that the monument was carved for him on behalf of the king as a token of his appreciation: our musician is on a par with the highest officials.

At the turn of the 6th Dynasty we know two such overseers of palace singers, both called Snefrunufer. They were possibly members of the same family, perhaps father and son. They had separate tombs at Saqqara but neither of these monuments has

73 Hekenu the harpist with Iti, her chironomist. Relief from the temple at Saqqara; 5th Dynasty. Egyptian Museum, Cairo (CG 1414).

any representations of musical activities. A namesake of theirs is known from a tomb at Giza, where his statue was found. He was in similar employment, but his actual title was 'instructor [sḥḏ] of singers in The Great House'. Musical employment in the palace was not a male prerogative: a woman could become 'overseer of female singers' and 'overseer of ladies in the harem'. A certain Hemtre held these titles. She had a tomb of her own, an unusual, though not unique state of affairs, but she had usurped it from a man, erasing his figure and replacing it with her own, adding her name and titles.

The duties of 'instructors' must have differed from those of the 'overseers'. We know of an 'instructor of singers' called Memi of the 5th Dynasty or later; a contemporary 'instructor of singers to the flute' by the name of Remeryptah; and, intriguingly, an 'instructor of the singers of the pyramid of King Userkaf' called Nikaure. This latter title opens up a whole new aspect of music-making. When and where would such pyramid singers perform? Or are we to take it that they actually sang in the palace, but were paid out of funds from the pyramid estate?

The discovery in recent years of the tomb of Nufer and Kaha near the causeway of King Unas at Saqqara has provided us with yet another title, namely that of 'director [ḥrp] of singers'. Both Nufer and Kaha, his father, were thus employed in the middle or late 5th Dynasty. In fact, many members of their family had a musical occupation. Kaha was both 'director' and 'instructor' of singers. He also held a title as priest of the 'southern Merit', the music goddess, and the inscriptions mention that he was 'unique' among the singers and had a beautiful voice. Nufer, as well as being director of singers, was also instructor in the royal artisans' workshops. Three of his sons were 'instructors of singers', and a fourth was 'director of singers in the palace'. Four other male relatives were 'instructors of singers', and two of them were also priests of Merit, a title which was perhaps honorific. The tomb of Nufer and Kaha is in a good state of preservation and, unusually for a musician's tomb, it depicts a musical ensemble entertaining the discerning owner.

By the beginning of the 6th Dynasty the flautist appears to gain greater prominence. A certain Ipi is named on his statue as 'flautist in The Great House' and a statuette of Senankhwer gives its owner's title simply as 'flautist'. In a provincial tomb at Meir in Middle Egypt a flautist is named, along with the two harp-playing daughters of the tomb owner.

It would seem that the tradition of secular music was maintained above all in the royal palace. To the titles 'overseer', 'instructor' and 'director' of musicians can be added a fourth, that of 'teacher' (sb3). A man named Rawer was 'teacher of the royal singers' in the 6th Dynasty. One would imagine that both the 'teacher' and the 'instructor' would have had to be active musicians themselves, teaching groups of musicians the technical side of their profession and acquainting them with the musical forms of the past, the basic structures on which they would then be able to elaborate and excel. Whether we can see in the 'directors' the chironomists known from Old Kingdom banquet ensembles remains an open question. The positions of 'director' and 'overseer' may have been purely administrative, and although familiarity with the subject would undoubtedly have been an advantage, it may not have been a prerequisite in Egyptian bureaucracy.

In the Middle Kingdom named musicians appear largely on stelae belonging to their patrons. Mention has already been made of Neferhotep, the blind harpist on

74 A priest giving lessons in sistrum-playing and hand-clapping. Tomb at Kom el-Hisn; Middle Kingdom.

the stela in Leiden (see chapter 7). The performers on a stela of a certain Renseneb are named as Ankhkhu, the harpist, and Duat, Isi . . . and Senebt, three ladies singing and clapping their hands. A songstress named Sathathor set up a memorial stela at Abydos which shows her being entertained by 'her beloved daughter Neferthotep-anket' on a harp decorated with an unusual animal's head. An offering formula on the stela, which would usually mention traditional gods, refers in this case to Merit, the music goddess.

The singers in the Middle Kingdom were properly trained to do their job. An 'overseer of prophets' and 'instructor of singers' called Khesuwer is shown on a wall of his tomb at Kom el-Hisn in the Delta giving lessons in hand-clapping and sistrum-playing. Ten ladies attend each class to develop their skills for their employment in the cult of Hathor in the local temple. It is from about this time that musicians and dancers performing in sacred places begin to be depicted. King Sesostris II of the 12th Dynasty regularly employed such people in a temple at Illahun, for a list of their attendance at the various feasts celebrated during the course of the year has survived on a fragile scroll of papyrus.

A tomb of the 18th Dynasty from Thebes has unusually copious information about the performers. The tomb belonged to Amenemhet, steward of the vizier of Tuthmosis III and it has two representations, which include three or four musical ensembles. One features a female harpist called Baket, a male lutenist, Amenemhet, and a female oboe-player named Ruiuresti; the lines of their song are also given. In the register below, the male harpist Bak is singing a joyful verse to Amun. On another wall we meet the harpist Ahmosi, who is accompanied by two named daughters of the tomb owner clapping their hands and joining in a song on the occasion of the New Year. Above them are represented the female oboe-player Kha-wet; a clapping girl called Kam; and a woman named as Mutnofret, who dances with two-handed clappers.

Contemporary 18th Dynasty tombs at Thebes abound in similar musical representations, but the names of the participants can rarely be established. The solo performer, however, usually the harpist, may be mentioned, as for example Amen-mosi in the tomb of Ineni (cf. chapter 7). Two harpists in the Middle Kingdom tomb of Antefoker were also commemorated (chapter 2), and in the tomb of a certain Seb-knakht at el-Kab three female singers are named.

During the New Kingdom and Late Period names of performers of sacred music are numerous (see chapter 3). Few are actually represented while playing an instrument, but one was Harwoz, the overseer of singers of Amun in the 25th Dynasty. He plays his harp and sings to a falcon-headed deity, though not to the god in whose employment he was supposed to be. Another was Zekhensef͑ankh, singer of Amun, playing to Re-Harakhti. Pedekhons, the chief lutenist of Khons, left a statue which shows him squatting with only his head emerging fully from the cubic form of the sculpture (a type known as a block or cube statue) (Plate 20). On the front was room for an inscription with his name and title, as well as a representation in relief showing him holding his instrument. Such a statue could have been set up in a temple.

To the title 'songstress' (ḥsyt) of a god or goddess is added another, šm͑yt, the specific title of the songstress of a deity. The distinction between the two is not immediately obvious. Both could play an instrument in addition to singing. A ḥsyt of Hathor, for example, is shown blowing her double oboe at a cult function, and the happy owner of a painted oboe-case was a šm͑yt of Mut. Countless ladies of the upper levels of society describe themselves as šm͑yt. Most frequently Amun is the god they serve, followed by Hathor, but this may be because of the abundance of monuments found at Thebes where the two deities were particularly popular. Such ladies were in a position to appear on their own monuments. Perhaps the most exquisite example is the statue of Meryt, wife of Maya, who was treasurer to Tutankhamun. The statue, showing Meryt clasping a *menat*, has long been in Leiden. The tomb of Maya and Meryt at Saqqara has recently been rediscovered, but it showed no further evidence of Meryt's musical activities.

It appears that musicians attached to the cult of a god were held in high esteem. They were in the unique position of being able to communicate with the deity and, through the singing of hymns, to keep his image alive. Some women came to have an influential position as 'divine adoratress' or 'god's wife of Amun'. However, there is evidence to suggest that some of the songstresses were of a different status. Abydos in Upper Egypt was a site of pilgrimage, for this was allegedly one of the burial places of Osiris himself. Ordinary Egyptians set up stelae at this site in order to benefit from the ceremonies carried out there; others were actually buried at his shrine. A section of the necropolis was set apart for songstresses (šm͑yt) of a number of deities (Osiris, Isis, Horus, Mut, Amun) and their stillborn children. It is not known why these women had a separate burial place. It may indicate a favoured status: perhaps it was a privilege for women dying in childbirth to be buried there. But the opposite may equally well be true; only one of the songstresses was accompanied by a husband, and possibly these women had no fathers in whose tombs they could be buried. Whatever the explanation, the burials indicate that chastity was not required for these musicians of the gods.

Literary sources suggest that some instruments were regarded more highly than others, and this would have applied to the players as well. A passage in a papyrus which laments the passing of old values and the general chaos of the present refers to the humble status of some instruments: 'He who was ignorant of a *dʒdʒt* now owns a harp [*bnt*]. He who could not sing now praises Merit'. The person to whom the authorship is attributed was himself a singer called Khakheperresenb. The first element of his name is identical to one of the names of King Sesostris II, so he must have been born after this king ascended the throne around 1878 BC. The state of confusion deplored in this text would refer to the situation in Egypt at the beginning of the First Intermediate Period. In quotations of this passage *dʒdʒt* has often been translated as 'lyre'. If this were correct, it would be most interesting, for it is just at this time that we first meet the lyre on Egyptian soil in the hands of a traveller, shown in a tomb at Beni Hassan. However, the word *dʒdʒwy* is known to have designated the player of the Ramesside arched harp, and there is no evidence whatsoever that the *dʒdʒt* was a lyre, which was otherwise called *knnr*. The implication of the passage is that the *dʒdʒt* was a modest instrument in comparison with the harp, and that it was made of wood (from the use of the determinative ⤳). From Middle Kingdom times or earlier the only feasible candidate would be a type of harp, unless the Egyptians confused their own terminology. This happened in more recent times when, in the Old Testament, the instrument to which David sang his hymns was persistently referred to as a harp when to all intents and purposes it was a lyre.

The reputations of other instruments might be tainted by unacceptable associations, as in the case of the oboe and lyre, which had distinctly erotic connotations (see chapter 8). The Egyptians of the 18th Dynasty had delighted in banquet ensembles which included both of these instruments, but a scribal school text of the 19th Dynasty advised against its pupils having anything to do with them.

The oboe and lyre had both been introduced into Egypt from abroad, and two other foreign-sounding instruments meet with the disapproval of the text's author: what may be a reed instrument (*wʒr*) and a wooden, possibly stringed instrument (*ntḫ?*). Perhaps we should put this down to the suspicion of a purist towards all foreign imports. In spite of this, however, the oboe, lute and lyre were well and truly accepted in Egypt, although other foreign imports have left less of an impression in the visual sources. Hand drums of the sort found at Avaris (see chapter 2) are represented only by a single wall-painting dating from just after the Amarna Period in a scene which is totally in the spirit of the art of Akhenaten. This type of drum remained an instrument of the people, and with the exception of the street scenes of Amarna art (see chapter 6) there was little occasion to depict it.

The evidence from el-Amarna shows that foreign musicians were welcomed at the court of Akhenaten, and some of the temple musicians employed by Sesostris II had also come from abroad. Just as foreign musicians came to Egypt and mingled in the highest circles, so it was also possible for Egyptian performers to go abroad. The

75 Songstress Henuttawi depicted on her own metal sistrum; 21st-26th Dynasty. Louvre (E 11201).

prince of Byblos, for example, enjoyed the services of an Egyptian songstress called Tentnau.[31] She was dispatched to cheer up the unfortunate Wenamun, who had been sent by the King of Egypt to secure a load of precious wood from Lebanon. He encountered endless problems and delays, and when the prince heard of this, he sent two measures of wine and a sheep, as well as his songstress to sing to him and chase away his gloomy thoughts. Perhaps she knew the same repertoire of love songs as her colleague Tashere, who was employed in the house of a mayor in Egypt (see p.111).

When pharaoh travelled, he would not be without his favourite musician. The harpist Amenemhab, called Mahu (see chapter 3), held the title of 'follower of the king in all foreign lands', and he would have been on the spot to entertain the king whenever he was overcome by sinister thoughts. Perhaps we should not be surprised to find royal persons themselves reaching for a musical instrument. There are numerous representations of queens shaking sistra. Ptolemaic queens are seen playing the crescent-shaped harp to a deity, and Ptolemy XII, father of Cleopatra, was himself an accomplished oboe-player, known as 'auletes'. His inspiration may have derived more from the Greeks than from the descendants of the ancient Egyptians, but nevertheless we can see in him the illustrious example of a long tradition of musical performers on Egyptian soil. The connection between the artist and his art is even more elusive in music than in literature, painting and sculpture, where the end product remains for us to see, along with some names of writers, scribes, painters and sculptors. The memory of great musicians lives on, but it requires an open mind to imagine their music.

10
The ancient traditions today

A cursory glance at a selection of modern Egyptian folk instruments betrays at once their evident debt to their Pharaonic ancestors. Some, indeed, are virtually identical in appearance, although there must be basic differences, such as the finer points of tuning. The changes which took place at the beginning of the Christian era and, later, with the Arab conquest had a profound impact on the arts and culture of Egypt. Art and architecture were transformed; in literature the outward form was altered when hieroglyphs went out of use, although some of the literary genres survived. Music, however, at least in as far as it was embodied in instruments, was carried into the new era, and even enjoyed a revival under the Arabs.

Egyptian customs spread widely, to neighbouring countries and further afield: in the Pharaonic Period we know of at least one Egyptian singer, Tentnau (mentioned above), at the court of Byblos in Syria. This connection continued into later times, for it was Syrian monks who brought the liturgy and music of the Egyptian Coptic Church to Ethiopia in the fifth century AD. Egyptian influence spread westwards too. Connections between peoples of Africa and Egypt and Berber tribesmen may have helped carry cultural currents across North Africa. In the oases of the Western Desert, notably at Siwa Oasis near the western edge of modern Egypt, Pharaonic influence is evident, not only in the remains of tombs and temples but also in certain customs of the modern inhabitants, who still betray their mixed origins. Even in Mauretania, on the far west of the continent, certain aspects of the musical tradition, with its Moorish roots, seem to echo Egyptian music as we know it from surviving instruments and the representations that we have inherited. It is therefore not just in Egypt itself that we must search for traces of ancient musical traditions, but in many other parts of Africa and the Middle East too.

The ancient instruments, and the music played on them, stood a good chance of surviving either if they became popular with the people, or if they came to play a part in sacred music, as for example in the church music of the Copts. This is the case with that archetypal religious instrument, the sistrum. It is maintained in use in the liturgy of the Ethiopian Copts as the instrument with which the priest points to the four corners of the world to demonstrate the extent of God's kingdom. It is also used as a solo instrument with otherwise unaccompanied songs. It has lost its ornaments, and become a simple rattle consisting of a metal frame with discs, but the sound it makes (strongly evoked by its name, *tsenatsil*), must be very similar to that produced by its ancient ancestor. The sistrum can be heard on recordings of the service in the rock churches of Lalibala in Ethiopia.

Cymbals, which appeared in various sizes towards the end of Pharaonic civilisation, are occasionally used in the church when incense is burnt, the tinkling sound of the censers mingling with the clashing of the cymbals. The instruments had previously been used in the cult of Dionysios, Cybele and Isis, largely in feasts of an orgiastic nature. The Copts may also use them at funerals, and they may have had a similar function in antiquity: an 18th Dynasty relief showing a funeral procession includes a woman who is possibly playing cymbals.

The round tambourine (*târ*) is frequently heard in Egypt, and rural wedding processions, for example, can still present scenes of celebration familiar from the monuments of the Pharaonic Period, where women wave branches, sing and beat tambourines or drums. In Nubia the tambourine is used to accompany both religious and secular songs, including love songs. The tambourine is primarily a folk instrument, although it does also make the occasional appearance in religious music, but in Egypt its popularity is overshadowed by the *darabukka*. Whenever a group of modern-day Egyptians go sailing on the river, or even take a bus excursion, one will bring a *darabukka* to liven up the proceedings. The repertoire of a belly dancer invariably contains an episode where she dances accompanied only by the *darabukka* player. The relationship between the two performers can even have an erotic force, and if well done it is a most alluring spectacle. The *darabukka* player can extract a great many different sounds from his instrument, depending on whether he hits the membrane in the centre (for deep notes) or on the edge (for high notes).

The barrel-shaped drum is found in many places in Africa. Of special interest is the use of the *kabaro* in certain ceremonies of the Coptic Church in Ethiopia, especially during the performance of some hymns. The singers hold a sistrum in one hand; in the other they have a 'prayer stick' which they move in a set pattern and throw into the air, all directed by the majestic rhythm of the large drum. In ancient Egypt the drum appears to occupy a border-line position between the secular and the sacred. The *kabaro* in Ethiopia, the *tabl*, its relative in the Islamic world, and the Turkish military *davul* are variants of the same basic instrument.

One of the most expressive instruments in Egyptian folk music is the *nây*, along with various relatives of different sizes. Made of reed, the *nây* has a bore of about 1.3 to 1.5cm, and its length varies between some 35 and 55cm. The shorter variants of the flute, known as *sibs*, *salamiya* and *uffata*, have wider bores. The *nây* has six finger-holes at the front and a thumb-hole halfway down the back, whereas the wider instruments have no thumb-hole. The flute used by the ancient Egyptians seems to have had the length of the modern *nây* and the width of the shorter flutes. Such instruments are a well-known feature of North African music, for example in Tunisia. The Egyptian *nây* has a range of two and a half octaves or more. Its sound quality varies from a deep hoarse tone at the bottom of its register, to a brighter, clearer timbre at the top, and is close in many ways to the human voice. The ancient flutes had fewer holes, and thus fewer notes, but the sound quality must have been very similar.

The modern *nây*, like its single-reed cousins in the clarinet family, is played with the use of circular breathing techniques. The *zummâra* and the *mashûra*, still used in folk music, appear to be modern equivalents of the ancient double clarinet (*mmt*). As we have seen (chapter 2), the vibrating reed of the *zummâra* is cut from below, whereas the *mashûra* reed is cut from above. The entire mouthpiece is taken into the player's mouth when the clarinet is in use. None of the ancient instruments have survived with mouthpieces, and so it is impossible to say which type of reed was in use. In fact, we can only surmise from the close similarity of ancient and modern instruments that the *mmt* was indeed an ancestor of this single-reed instrument. A Coptic double clarinet of the seventh century AD allegedly had a single-reed mouthpiece more or less *in situ* when found, so that its use does seem to go back beyond the Middle Ages at least. The *zummâra* has five double finger-holes on the front, the smaller *mashûra* just four. On both ancient and modern instruments the holes are slightly displaced, indicating that perfect tuning in unison was not intended. In present-day Egypt another version, the *arghûl*, has one short tube and one very long one, which acts as a drone. The sound is rich and raw, and it would always be the dominant instrument in an ensemble.

In contrast to the clarinet, the modern Egyptian oboe or shawm, *mizmâr*, bears little resemblance to the ancient version, for it is a single instrument, made of wood with a conical bore. It is usually played in popular ensembles along with a couple of spiked fiddles (*rebâba*). The instrument has an extremely penetrating sound.

76 Modern Egyptian *nây*. L. *c.* 35cm.

77 Modern Egyptian *zummâra*. L. *c.* 35cm.

A trumpet in use in Morocco, the *nafîr*, bears a striking resemblance to those from the tomb of Tutankhamun, except that it may be longer, up to 1.7m. It produces just one note, which is heard in wedding processions.

In our search for modern survivals of that most Egyptian of instruments, the harp, we must once again leave Egyptian soil. A small version of a shovel-shaped harp is allegedly played among the Bisharin, a bedouin tribe south of Aswan, many of whose customs are similar to those of the ancient Egyptians. Among African harps the *ennanga* of Uganda, with a curved neck and five strings, has several features in common with the shovel-shaped harp. The *ardin*, played by Mauretanian women, on the other hand, has a straight neck and a sound-box made of a calabash, covered with a membrane. It has about ten strings. In appearance these folk instruments would seem to be related to the harps played by the ancient Egyptians, but concerning the vital question of tuning we are none the wiser.

The lyre (*simsimîya* or *tanbûra*), is still much used in the southern part of Egypt on the borders of Sudan. A simple version has a deep metal plate covered with a membrane as its sound-box, and arms of equal length. The method of playing seems very close to that shown on the monuments: one hand strikes all the strings with a plectrum while the fingers of the other hand are spread out behind the plane of the strings, deadening the ones which are not to sound. In Ethiopia a wooden lyre (*bogana*), was in use until recently for vocal accompaniment, but only in the royal family during religious ceremonies. This instrument is generally taken to be the 'harp of David' from the Old Testament. It is about 75cm high, with five or ten strings.

Apart from the rounded shape of its sound-box, it is very reminiscent of the giant lyres of the Amarna Period and those played in the Ptolemaic temple of Hathor at Philae.

The Copts made use of the long-necked lute in their music. They changed the shape of its sound-box, carving it out of one piece of wood and giving it a clearly waisted shape. A number of such instruments dating from the fourth to the eighth century AD have survived; these were provided with three or four strings. The Arabic *tanbûr* shares some of the characteristics of the Pharaonic and Coptic lutes, especially in having a long neck and three strings. In Egyptian classical music a short-necked lute is now in use, but the long-necked version is known from many areas of the Middle East. In Mauretania men still play a long lute called *tidinit*, which is reminiscent of the ancient Egyptian instrument. It has an oval or waisted sound-box made of wood and covered with a membrane. The four strings are tied with leather rings around the neck, and at the opposite end they are fastened to the extension of the neck, which passes through the body. The tuning is adjusted by moving the leather rings, just as an Egyptian lute-player would have tuned the strings of his instrument by moving the tasselled pieces of string with which they were fastened. The music played on this lute, and on the Mauretanian harp mentioned above, belongs to the repertoire of Moorish classical music. In other parts of the Islamic world the long lute is also widely used in secular music.

The musical traditions and techniques of these instruments, with their roots in the distant past, merit study, for they offer us clues about how to interpret the evidence from Egypt. It must be emphasised, however, that many kinds of music can be played on one instrument, and this is only a possible approach, not a final interpretation. These reservations apply in particular to the use of the human voice in music, for the ancient evidence is sparse indeed. However, despite the perils of such an exercise, it is still worth undertaking it in our attempt to flesh out the otherwise dry bones of academic evidence and bring to life the music of the past.

The most obvious source is, again, Coptic liturgical music, for the Copts have maintained traditions which in other circumstances may well have died out. These practices have survived particularly well in Ethiopia. The creation of liturgical music is accredited to a monk named Yared who lived in northern Ethiopia around AD 600. The church singers make extensive use of the guttural sounds of Ge'ez. A group of them will sing in unison, but not necessarily following the same time. Combined with a rich though not polyphonic mixture of different voices and individual ornamentations on the basic tune, the impression to Western ears is of an inaccuracy of tuning. As we have seen in earlier chapters, ancient Egyptian musicians appear to have aimed for a similar effect in their instrumental music.

In Egypt itself the church singer uses a gesture which is very similar to one

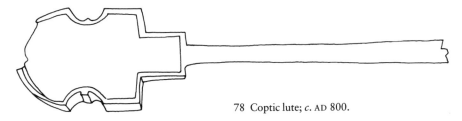

78 Coptic lute; *c.* AD 800.

employed by the ancient singers: while performing, he places his hand over his chin next to his ear. Allegedly this is to emphasise his voice, but only he himself would benefit from this illusion: inside his head his voice will seem louder. With his other hand he will perform gestures which are again reminiscent of those of the ancient chironomists. The explanation given is that they are used for teaching purposes in order to make students memorise the pieces. Some are rhythmic, others demonstrate melodic movements. The singing and the gestures are as closely linked as they were in ancient times, when the word 'to sing' was accompanied by the determinative of a human arm. The Coptic singer employs a nasal tone, and it is a characteristic of this style of singing to extend a single syllable almost indefinitely, presenting it in a richly ornamented melodic passage before it is followed by the rest of the word.

When we come to consider how the singers and instrumentalists combined their skills, the music of Mauretania may again offer some pointers, for here we seem to find further parallels with ancient Egypt, although caution is needed to avoid over-interpreting the evidence. The classical music of Mauretania is performed exclusively by professional musicians, the 'griots', who hand down their skills orally from one generation to another. All griots sing. In addition, women play the harp and men the lute, but they do not necessarily make use of both voice and instrument in performance, if they feel that their true talent lies in a particular field. The music is based on a complicated musical theory, combining modal systems and melodic and rhythmical structures. The modes, or 'ways', are three in number, called 'black', 'white' and 'spotted'. Each can lead to other 'ways', every single one of which is characterised by a set of melodic or rhythmic outlines. Each 'way' is connected with a specific occasion or mood.

When a performance is about to begin, the griots will tune their instruments and prepare themselves and their audience for the chosen 'way'. The singer will hum some lines, and he will repeat the note which is the first step of the 'way'. Here we are reminded of the Egyptian chironomists, persistently demonstrating to the musicians, and to us, one particular note or interval, which must have formed the basis of the performance. After this mixed instrumental and vocal introduction, the singer takes

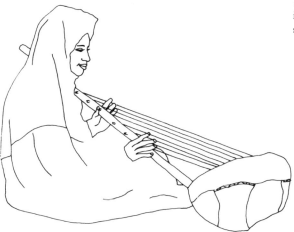

79 Moorish female griot playing an ardin, a harp with eight strings.

80 Scene of street celebration with trumpet and tambourine. Relief from a temple at el-Amarna; 18th Dynasty. Norbert Schimmel Collection, New York.

over, or two singers perform alternately, accompanied by the instruments. Towards the end the rhythmic accompaniment predominates. The women beat the membranes of the sound-boxes of their harps and clap their hands. The singer will then continue and perhaps break into another 'way', at which point another instrumental introduction is required.

In the area of popular music, evidence from many parts of the Middle East can also help us to understand methods of performing in the distant past. As we have seen above, occasions celebrated in traditional style, such as weddings, can be matched remarkably closely with scenes of rejoicing on the monuments, where processions of women and children wave branches, sing and beat drums or tambourines. The tradition of women playing tambourines in processions appears to be firmly rooted in the Middle East. Interestingly, it has been reported of certain close-knit Jewish communities that women's songs in such situations follow the motions of the group rather than the text, exhibiting a characteristic rising and falling movement. Drumbeats come at regular intervals, falling on each period of the melody, thus marking its conclusion rather than dividing it into bars. It is not unlikely that the Egyptian women shown rejoicing in such scenes are following similar customs; their chant may have made use of certain notes suited to specific movements, such as raising their arms, waving branches, advancing or receding. This exercise would possibly have been punctuated by passages of cheerful drum-beats. Such a use of rhythm to break up a melodic line is known in other traditional societies, as for example among certain American Indian peoples. Clapping hands indicates that the singing has to stop.

The attempt to retrace the musical past of an ancient people through its silent monuments and artefacts can be compared to interpreting inarticulate prehistoric civilisations. We can present the evidence, suggest its function and meaning, compare it with practices elsewhere and refer it to our own Western background. The possibility remains that the truth will elude us, in detail or in full. The careful examination of all the material by scholars and experts in a variety of fields, evaluating the evidence and considering its implications, offers us the only hope that the music of the ancient Egyptians can sound again, if in our imagination alone.

Notes

1 Plato, *Laws* (trans. R. G. Bury). Loeb edition, 1967.

2 For musical notation in various civilisations, see A. Machabey, *La notation musicale*. Paris, 1971.

3 Hymn from Dendara: H. Junker, 'Poesie der Spätzeit', in *Zeitschrift für ägyptische Sprache* 43, 190g, p.101ff.

4 E.g. Kaplony in *Chronique d'Égypte* 44, 1969, p.27ff; Altenmüller in *Chronique d'Égypte* 48, 1973, p.211.

5 L. Manniche, *Lost Tombs. A study of certain eighteenth dynasty monuments in the Theban necropolis*, ch.5. London and New York, 1988.

6 Plutarch, *Lives. Antony,* xxxvi (trans. B. Perrin). Loeb edition, 1968. Instruments, trans. LM.

7 M. Bietak, 'Eine "Rhytmusgruppe" aus der Zeit des späten Mittleren Reiches: ein Beitrag sur Instrumentenkunde des Alten Ägypten', in *Jahresheften des Österreichischen archäologischen Institutes*, Bd. LVI, 1985, pp.3–18.

8 Tomb of Rekhmire (No.100) at Thebes.

9 Tomb of May (No.130) at Thebes.

10 Tomb of Nebamun at Thebes, now British Museum 37984, Manniche, op. cit., p.142.

11 Tomb of Kenamun (No. 93) at Thebes.

12 Diodorus of Sicily I.16.1 (trans. C.H. Oldfather). Loeb edition, 1968.

13 Athenaeus, *Deipnosophistai* IV, 174b, 'It is not like the single-pipe, which is so common among you Alexandrians, which causes pain to the listeners rather than any musical delight,' trans. C. B. Gulick. Loeb edition, 1957; id. 175d for a reference to the work of Juba II on the 'monaulos', also called 'the reed'. The following paragraphs contain interesting references to other instruments in use in Alexandria at the time.

14 Diodorus I.18.4.

15 I.E.S. Edwards (ed.), *Hieroglyphic Texts from Egyptian Stelae etc. in the British Museum*, Vol.8, pl.30, p.35–6. London, 1939.

16 C. Kuentz in *Recueil d'études égyptologiques dédiées à la mémoire de Jean-François Champollion*, pp.601–10. Paris, 1922.

17 E. Drioton, *Rapport sur les fouilles de Médamoud (1926). Les inscriptions.*, pp.26–8. Cairo, 1927.

18 Tomb No.82 at Thebes.

19 Apuleius, *Metamorphoses* XI, 4 (trans. J. Arthur Hanson). Loeb edition, 1989.

20 Athenaeus. op. cit. 497d-e.

21 Clemens Alexandrinus, *Exhortation to the Greeks*, ch.II. 14p (trans. G. W. Butter-worth). Loeb edition, 1960.

22 Tomb No.112 at Thebes.

23 N. de G. Davies, *The Rock Tombs of El Amarna* VI, p.29. London, 1908.

24 Ibid. IV, p.28.

25 For harpers' songs, see M. Lichtheim, 'The songs of the harper', in *Journal of Near Eastern Studies* IV, 1945, p.178ff.

26 Ibid., pp.104–5, pls III, V.

27 Diodorus I.81.7

28 For the complete text, cf. L. Manniche, *Sexual Life in Ancient Egypt*, p.80–1. London and New York, 1987.

29 Herodotus II.60 (trans. A. D. Godley). Loeb edition, 1946.

30 H. Junker, *Das Götterdekret über das Abaton*, pp.21, 31. Vienna, 1913.

31 W.K. Simpson (ed.), *The Literature of Ancient Egypt*, p.154. New Haven and London, 1973.

List of museums holding important Egyptian musical instruments

Ägyptisches Museum
Schlossstrasse 70
1000 Berlin 19
Germany

Egyptian Museum
Midan el-Tahrir
Cairo
Egypt

Museo Archeologico
Piazza Santissima Annunziata
Florence
Italy

Rijksmuseum van Oudheden
Rapenburg 28
2400 Leiden
The Netherlands

British Museum
Great Russell Street
London WC1B 3DG
UK

Metropolitan Museum of Art
Fifth Avenue at 82nd Street
New York, NY 10028
USA

Musée du Louvre
Palais du Louvre
75041 Paris 1
France

Bibliography

Major works on ancient Egyptian music:

ANDERSON, R. D. *Catalogue of Antiquities in the British Museum III. Musical Instruments*. London, 1976.

HICKMANN, E., and MANNICHE, L. 'Altägyptische Musik', in *Neues Handbuch der Musikwissenschaft*, vol.II, ch.II, pp.31–75. Laaber, 1989.

HICKMANN, H. *Catalogue général des antiquités égyptiennes du Musée du Caire. Instruments de musique*. Cairo, 1949.

HICKMANN, H. *Musicologie pharaonique*. Kehl, 1956.

HICKMANN, H. *Musikgeschichte in Bildern. Ägypten*. Leipzig/Halle, 1961.

HICKMANN, H. *45 siècles de musique dans l'Égypte ancienne*. Paris, 1956.

Vies et travaux. I. Hans Hickmann [collected papers published by the Egyptian Antiquities Organization]. Cairo, 1980.

MANNICHE, L. *Ancient Egyptian Musical Instruments* (*Münchner ägyptologische Studien 34*). Munich, 1975.

MANNICHE, L. *Musical Instruments from the Tomb of Tut'ankhamun* (*Tut'ankhamun's Tomb Series* VI). Oxford, 1976.

SACHS, C. *Die Musikinstrumente des alten Ägyptens*. Berlin, 1921.

SACHS, C. *The History of Musical Instruments*. London, 1942.

SACHS, C. *The Rise of Music in the Ancient World East and West*. London, 1944.

SCHAEFFNER, A. *Origine des instruments de musique*. Paris, 1968.

ZIEGLER, C. *Les instruments de musique égyptiens au Musée du Louvre*. Paris, 1979.

Recent papers relevant to the present work:

MANNICHE, L. 'The erotic oboe', in *The Archaeology of Early Music Cultures*. Proceedings of the 3rd meeting of the ICTM-Study Group on Music Archaeology, Hannover/Wolfenbüttel 1986, pp.189–98. Düsseldorf, 1988.

MANNICHE, L. 'Symbolic blindness', in *Chronique d'Égypte* 53, pp.13–21, 1978.

MANNICHE, L. 'Á la cour d'Akhenaton et de Nefertiti', in *Les Dossiers d'Archéologie* 142, Nov. 1989, pp.24–31.

Recordings relevant to the present work:

HICKMANN, H., and CARL GREGOR, HERZOG ZU MECKLENBURG. *Catalogue d'enregistrements de musique folklorique égyptienne.* Strasbourg/Baden-Baden 1958. With LP record.

DRAFFKORN, A., CROCKER, R. L., and BROWN, R. R. *Sounds from Silence. Recent Discoveries in Ancient Near Eastern Music.* Berkeley [1980?]. With LP record.

Index

Egyptian words